Three Apache Arrows

To Anna
" Happy Trails "

Doyle Renolds

Doyle Renolds

BLACK ROSE
writing™

ISBN: 978-1-61296-366-2

PUBLISHED BY BLACK ROSE WRITING

www.blackrosewriting.com

Printed in the United States of America

Three Apache Arrows is printed in Palatino Linotype

To Jack Grant 1939 – 2011
My Uncle, my brother, my best friend.
Thanks for always being there for me.

Three Apache Arrows

Chapter 1

It was a morning to die for, and with the Apache arrow stuck in my chest it could happen. Aside from that, I've got plenty of shade, water, and a nice soft rock for a pillow. What more could a man want? For starters, you could get rid of those damned Apaches who have me holed up in these rocks. But it's doubtful I can talk them into leaving without my horse and scalp, and I've grown attached to both.

Before sunup this morning, I was breaking camp and enjoying a pot of sour mash coffee. The blues and purples of the night sky were evolving into the pink and orange of dawn, when I heard the whinny of ponies nearby. They must have caught the scent of my buckskin on the morning breeze. They could have been wild, but I didn't think so.

I had mustered out of the Confederate army in Virginia six months ago. Like every other battered and broken Civil War veteran, on both sides, I was glad to see the conflict over and traveling home. At least I was one of those who still had a home. We'd experienced the horrors of war, and now only wanted to forget them. Making a few miles a day, I was returning to New Mexico and former life on my ranch. A man sees too many things nightmares are made of in a war, and has to find his own healing place. It's somewhere he can close his eyes, and only see the inside of his eyelids. The war wasn't the glorious adventure a lot of men thought it would be. That bastard Sherman told it like it was. I'd emerged from hell physically intact with my horse and guns, and was grateful I had done so.

I drifted south from Virginia into the Carolinas. In the middle of Georgia I turned west, crossing Alabama and Mississippi, then rode a ferryboat across the Big Muddy. Traveling north of bayou country, I counted the miles, and each day brought me closer to home. There was abundant kindness from strangers on the roads since the war ended, and a lot of men in need of it. I'd said a lot of thank you's and meant every one.

Most of the journey was now behind me. Texas started out green in the east and led to wind and dust on the western plains. In front of me lay; miles of thorny cactus, mesquite, rattlesnakes, and Indians, some friendly, but mostly not. Texas is a big territory with plenty of elbow room. The Kiowas and Apaches go their own way until someone fires them up and pushes them down the warpath, or they see some easy pickings, like me traveling alone. Comanches, on the other hand are ornery as snakes anytime, especially if they find you in their territory, and I was crossing the southern edge of it. I planned to stay south of Comancheria, and ride lonesome through the Indian territories. It was a good plan while it lasted.

I had chopped wood, and done chores for farm houses along the way, to earn meals and traveling grub. I held onto my guns at the surrender: a pair Navy Colts I'd brought into the war and a Henry repeating rifle I purchased in Virginia. They were all superior weapons. Aside from my guns, the buckskin I was riding and the contents of my saddlebags were all the possessions I had with me, not counting the gray and butternut uniform and great coat I wore.

I let my horse graze when he could and kept our water bags full. There was a bag of oats in the saddlebags for him when the grass got scarce, and a bag of beans for me when game was hard to find. And a few other necessities.

I heard the ponies again. Ponies meant Indians. They were probably Apache, but being this close to Comanche territory it could be either. Even so, I could count on it being trouble since they were traveling near their tribal borders. They must have crossed my trail at dusk yesterday, and camped close by, anticipating the addition of my scalp to their collection this morning.

I'd pushed hard yesterday to make camp before dark at a tall butte I saw in the distance. It was larger and further away than it looked. I'm glad I kept going, considering the uninvited guests who would have arrived before dark.

I had the options of a fast start out of here, or to hole up and wait them out, or I could meet them head on going out in a blaze of glory like a dime novel hero. The last one wasn't going to happen, I'd seen too many men wasted with that horse droppings bravado during the war. Too many brave men's lives were squandered on blind courage.

As quiet as possible, I saddled the buckskin and loaded my supplies and bedroll. I left the coals glowing in the small campfire. I hated to leave my coffeepot, especially when it was full of sour mash coffee. It was too hot to take with me, and not worth my scalp waiting for it to cool off.

It was a long ride to any cover from the butte, and there was no way my buckskin was going to outrun Indian ponies across desert plains. After I made camp yesterday, I had taken a walk around the butte at twilight, and found an opening in the rocks which led into a small canyon filled with cactus, dead trees, and a small pond. If it hadn't been so close to dark I would have camped there. A man could hold up there for a long time if he had to...and I had to.

I led the buckskin through the canyon opening, and staked him on a patch of grass away from the entrance. I eased back out of the rocks to take a look. Yep, I'd left just in time. There were three young Mescalero Apaches milling around the campfire looking for sign. Those boys were young, but I had seen what they could do, not unlike the soldiers their age and younger who'd fought like wildcats in the war. I needed to prepare for their visit. In a matter of minutes, they would be able to see well enough to follow my tracks to the canyon.

They would come afoot because a horse would have to be walked into the canyon. The sheer rock walls of the butte prevented them from climbing to attack from above. These things were in my favor.

I hauled several big rocks to the canyon entrance, and set them on the ground about a foot apart to keep me from being rushed. I hid behind a stand of cholla cactus and waited. I set my pistols and a box of shells on the rock next to me. My rifle in my lap and a canteen close by. When the party started, I was ready to dance.

After waiting the best part of the morning, I wondered what was taking my quests so long to arrive. When the answer came to me, I almost laughed out loud. They had found my pot of sour mash coffee. The situation was about to change, and if I was careful, I could have some fun.

Let me tell you how I make that wonderful concoction. First, I get a coffee pot half full of water and coffee, boil it, and then take it off the fire. After it sits a few minutes for the grounds to settle, I fill the rest of the pot with good old southern sour mash bourbon. It gets you moving in the mornings, and hushes the yelling in your sleep. I have taken quite a liking to it since the war ended. Those jugs in my saddlebags helped fade the memories of what I had seen on the battlefields.

Suddenly, I heard a war whoop, and a warrior charged through the entrance to the canyon. He saw me, lifted his bow and let an arrow fly. Simultaneously, I fired a shot aimed at the rock wall above his head. The bullet made a loud ricochet and peppered him with rock chips. He cried out and turned tail back out of the canyon. He probably thought he had been shot. He was damn good with a bow, the arrow was sticking in the right side of my chest. The good news was my great coat and pants suspender had stopped most of it.

The arrow was worrisome, but no time to fret over it now. I broke the shaft off and tossed it aside. I hung the great coat on a small dead tree close to me, and set my hat above, barely having time to slide low behind the cactus. The other two Indians, bleary eyed and filled with whiskey courage, made a staggering run through the rocks towards me. They each loosed an arrow in the direction of my coat and hat, while I peppered the rocks around them with both of my pistols.

With bullets ricocheting around them like a swarm of bees, they ran in a full drunken panic. They stumbled over the boulders I'd set in the path, and they both hit the ground hard. For a second I thought I'd hit them, but realized they were both knocked out cold. This had been fun, but I'd better be careful, for there was a fresh scalp hanging on one of their belts.

I crept past the two boys to the canyon entrance, and spied the third Indian standing at the remains of my campfire. He held the coffeepot to his lips, draining the rest of my sour mash coffee. Good. I dragged his friends back through the rocks to the canyon opening. I took a full jug of whiskey from my saddlebag and poured some on my wound. It smarted a mite. I drank a long pull from the jug, and left it on the ground between the unconscious Apaches.

I could make a run for it, but I had an idea, and if I were careful, I would have a lot more fun. And maybe even get my coffeepot back.

A few minutes later I could hear someone tentatively calling out in Apache, probably the names of the two unconscious boys. As they regained consciousness, moans and groans turned to excited talk. They had discovered the jug. It would be a long day for me, but when I rode out of here, I wouldn't have anyone trailing me with blood in their eye.

While they were discovering the pleasure inside that clay jug, I needed to attend to the arrow in my chest. The arrowhead wasn't very deep, not much more than its length. There was enough of the shaft left to grip. The arrow had struck the muscle just above my right breast, and hadn't hit any of my vitals. I lit a match and sterilized my knife blade. Using the blade tip I worked the arrowhead barbs out of the flesh, and soon removed the whole piece. I used a strip of cloth I had cut from my only clean shirt to make a compress, and held it tight against the wound until the bleeding stopped. I tied another strip around my shoulder to hold the bandage in place. A sawbones would have done a lot better job, but I had seen men survive worse medical attention given in the field.

It was a long hot day, but I didn't receive any more attention from my new friends. Toward dusk I could hear some chanting and singing. I crept to the canyon entrance, and peered out to be certain my jug of whiskey was put to good use. The Apache boys were having an Indian fandango. They danced around a large fire, whooping it up and feeling no pain.

I waited and watched until twilight, and figured it was time. I fetched my great coat and the arrows fired at it, one had even hit it, I broke them in half along with the shaft of the one that hit me. I poked them through the front of the coat, and attached them on the inside with a small branch so they wouldn't fall out, and put it on along with my hat. I rubbed a pinch of flour on my face and I was ready. I walked out of the rocks.

Waving my arms, I approached the campfire from the dark and let out a rebel yell, accompanied by a WHOOOOOOO! Those three Apache boys saw me, and ran like the hounds of hell were after them, or in their minds, something even worse. Screeching and terrified they wouldn't stop until they ran out of steam, or into something solid. Believing in the supernatural as they do, the whiskey would only enhance those fears.

I knew they would sober up in the morning and return, so I

left them another surprise. I spread my great coat out on the sand, and removed the stick inside the shafts were attached to. I pushed the shafts through the coat into the ground, and placed my hat where my head would be. I wished I could be here to see the look on their faces when they came back, but I planned to be miles away by then. Laughing to myself, I grabbed my coffeepot and rode away.

Life can be very good sometimes.

* * *

Aieee!!! Pony Stealer and Stone Knife must be right. It was a Ganh, a mountain spirit, we angered. I thought it might have been the Coyote Man playing tricks on us, but he would have killed us when we drank the whiskey. Aieee! My head still hurts. We must have angered the Ganh by entering his home, so He sent the soldier ghost to warn us away. When we returned to beg forgiveness at dawn, all that was left of Him was sand. His coat still held my arrows. My friends are poor shots, and lost all their arrows, but the ones I gave them flew true. They were all stuck in his chest. We must never anger this spirit again. What a story we have to tell when we reach our village.

Life can be very good sometimes.

Chapter 2

My horse was as tired as I after several hours of walking with me in the saddle. A fingernail moon had risen, but the going was slow in the sparse light, having to dodge rocks and cactus. We needed to find a place to homestead for the remainder of the night. I was watching our back trail for shadows coming over the rises behind us, but had seen nothing. I figured it was safe enough to stop and rest for the night.

We wandered into a wide arroyo which narrowed some as the sides got steeper. Soon it was deep enough for us to get out of the wind and bed down for the night. I fed and watered the buckskin after taking his saddle off and giving him a good rub down. The night was cool, but not cold, and even though my mind was spinning after the events of the day, nothing would keep me awake as tired as I was.

I had picked up a rock in one of my worn out boots, which made me limp for a couple of steps after climbing down out of the saddle. I shucked both boots since the creek bed had a sandy bottom. I was already thinking about sleeping on that bed of sand, soft as a feather bed. I unrolled my bedroll and put it to good use.

Sometime in the night I was awakened by something, not sure what. I lay there and listened, pistol in hand, for several minutes. Then I realized what it was. All the night sounds were missing. Around me all was quiet and still, without an insect

chirping, a coyote howl, or even the wind wailing. I experienced
a tornado once, and the stillness moments before it hit reminded
me of this.

As anyone who has traveled the desert lands can tell you, it's
a strange and unusual place, where unexplainable things
happen, and you are only wasting your time trying to explain
them to anyone who hasn't been there. Over the far hills I saw a
glow as bright as the full moon, moving from left to right, then
back again. Then it was gone and the dark returned with
millions of stars. A coyote concert commenced in the distance.
In another place, I would have been spooked by this, but not in
the desert. Here it was just another event of nature I accepted
rather than questioned. Strange lights weren't anything new
here, along with many other strange things. Northeast of here
the Indians talk of a giant cave guarded by thousands of bats,
and I had ridden to the giant sand dunes west of the ranch,
where a man would think he was in the Sahara desert. Everyone
in the territory knew the legends of Ruidosa's healing places,
and many afflicted people travel there seeking cures. For
hundreds of miles this was a strange and magical area. In Taos
there stands a giant pueblo, legends say it has been there over a
thousand years, built by whom no one knows.

Whatever had awakened me bade me no harm, and now
was gone. Fireballs, freak lightning, or something else? Only the
old gods of the desert knew for sure and they ain't talking.

I slid back in my bedroll and slept until that little period
before dawn, when the demons of war came charging into my
dreams to torment me with visions of the past. Once again I
smelled the powder smoke, heard grown men missing pieces of
themselves screaming, and young boys crying for the mamas
they would never see again.

I woke up covered in a cold sweat. Sleep was done for this
night. I threw the blanket aside, my body shaking like I was
riding a buckboard wagon with a bad wheel. I sat with my head

in my hands. My poor horse stared at me. I wonder if he has similar dreams.

I couldn't risk a campfire. Dawn found me with a piece of deer jerky between my teeth and doing the morning chores. Tending to my horse first, I watered him and gave him a few oats for a treat. I stripped my guns down, then cleaned and oiled them. I checked the loads in each. If I have to shoot you, I want you to be shot.

I looked at my worn army boots standing tall in the sand, not unlike two old troopers waiting for the morning march to commence. From their appearance, it was evident we had traveled many a mile on rocky roads. I probably didn't look much better with my shaggy hair and beard, and a well-worn uniform or at least the pieces I still had left of it.

I picked up the boot with the rock caught in the sole. I would patch it as best I could. A man needs a pair of boots in the desert, and even old ones are better than none. A man is always stepping on cactus and lava rocks, or worse: something crawling with sharp teeth.

I started digging in the boot sole with my knife, and experienced an event that would change my life forever. The rock I pried out was a solid gold nugget, worth more money than I had seen in a year. There was only one place I could have acquired it. Last night when I left the butte, I had mounted my horse, and not touched the ground again until I stopped here to camp.

I reckon I have plenty to study on this morning.

Chapter 3

The shadows on the inside and outside of my mind vanished, as dawn broke over the ridges back to the east. I had been prepared to continue my journey home, and to meet whatever challenges awaited me there. I left a Mexican family to tend the ranch and my few head of cattle. They also looked after my niece, Charley, as I had done since she was a child. Charley, short for Charlene, was my niece. She was more of a Charley and more of a daughter than a niece.

Like many frontier children, she had lost both parents during the Comanche raids before the war. They were buried on my ranch in a small plot under the cottonwoods, next to my wife. My brother-in-law Josh had made the raiding party pay dearly, and bought my sister Anne and Charley enough time to escape, before the Comanches killed him. They made it to my ranch, and my sister Anne, like my beloved Meg, would never leave it.

Painful, but tolerable, I cleaned and dressed my arrow wound, then changed into some clean underwear and a linen shirt. I sat on a rock and tugged my boots on. I pulled the nugget out of my pocket and examined it.

It was pure and shiny in the morning sun. There was only one place I could have picked it up. I hadn't dismounted until I stopped here last night, and that nugget in my boot had been worrying me before I mounted my horse back at the butte. The ranch could wait a couple more days.

I'm not a greedy man by nature, but with the war over money was going to be mighty scarce, especially for the south. A couple more of those nuggets would be enough to get the ranch in shape with a nice nest egg left over for hard times.

I headed back in the direction I traveled the night before, and the morning sun was blinding. I rode with my head down and my eyes looking at the ground, wishing I had my hat back. I easily retraced the buckskin's tracks, and after a couple of hours the sun had risen to a tolerable height for facing east. I could see the butte standing tall in the distance, and reined my horse straight at it. I also checked my long gun in case my Apache friends wanted to play some more.

I was cautious, and took my time approaching by a roundabout route. I looked for Indian sign, and found the tracks of three unshod ponies heading south towards Mexico. I hope those boys continued moving in that direction. Tugging on the reins, I headed for my previous campsite.

As I approached the campsite, I could see my greatcoat still staked to the ground with those three Apache arrows and it made me smile. There had been plenty of foot traffic around it, but none on it. It must have spooked those boys pretty good.

I pulled the arrow shafts out of the coat. I had the arrowheads in my pocket. Souvenirs for Charley.

The morning winds across the desert blew chill, I draped my old coat over my shoulders, fastened the neck clasp, and grabbed my hat off the ground.

I searched the area around the campfire, and looked for anything shiny or yellow, but found nothing. Pulling the buckskin by his reins, I walked him back through the passageway of our little canyon. He remembered the patch of grass inside and trotted along next to me, eager to graze. I tethered him there after he had a long drink of water from the pond.

The cholla and prickly pear cactus were heavy in some places, making my prospecting a little difficult, but I was in no hurry. I was still empty handed when I found a crevice in the canyon wall. It was large enough for a man to pass through, but overgrown with cactus. I had ridden all the way back here, I might as well be thorough. This little box canyon was the only other place I could have picked up the nugget.

Not wanting to be a pincushion, I pulled a branch off a dead tree and parted the cactus, pushing the sharp needled limbs aside without having to beat them down. It was a lot less work, while letting those cactus still make a living doing whatever cactus do. My coat protected me from the needles sufficiently, and watching for anything that might bite or sting, I made it to the crevice. I looked down and saw I wasn't the first person to pass through the opening.

Facing me were steps cut out of the rock and they led upward. Some were covered with sand a couple of inches deep. They were ancient, and protected from the elements by the rock overhang. No one had trod here in ages.

It had taken a lot of time and effort to carve those steps out of the rock wall. For what purpose? Taking a long look at those steps, my mind wandered down several paths. None that made any sense. Feeling like an intruder, I put my foot on the first step and the hairs on the back of my neck stood up. I ascended the steps, continuing up and following the inside wall of the butte, with an occasional landing built in the gaps between the rocks, which allowed light in and a view out. I could see for miles, and I was far from the top of the steps.

I hadn't believed in hootie haints since I was a boy, but this place gave me a feeling like you might get walking in a cemetery after dark, and followed by something you wouldn't want to catch up to you. I've had similar feelings walking into an ambush. If it wasn't for the gold nugget in my pocket, I think I would turn around start back down those steps.

I had to see what lay at the top. I loosened the hammer strap on my holster before continuing the last steep incline. Above me, I could see blue sky and an opening in the rocks. I wanted to hurry, but luckily for me, caution won out over curiosity. When I reached the top, I was overwhelmed by the panoramic view before me. I must have been able to see fifty miles, but I was more concerned with the skeleton lying in front of me. It appeared to grin, like I was an old friend he had been waiting for.

His bones lay on the stone floor in front of me, intertwined with dozens of rattlesnakes, all looking at me. I was probably the first visitor they had ever seen. I was glad I hadn't rushed head long into the welcoming committee.

There was a courtyard facing the landing I was standing on. It was partially uncovered from the rock overhang, which allowed sunlight to warm the open area. Natural rock walls at the cliff's edge offered protection from a long fall to the rocks below, and made it impossible to see any of this from the ground. A person could stand watch here and observe everything for miles in all directions. Three hallways led off the courtyard into the butte itself. I would have to explore these.

First, I had to turn into a snake charmer. Fortunately for me, cool weather makes rattlesnakes as docile as they ever get, and the day hadn't warmed yet. This was the reason they were puddled together in the sun. I still held the branch I was using as a walking stick, and I started scooping them up with the end of the branch. I pitched the ill-tempered bastards over the side of the cliff, several at a time. It was a good thing for me they didn't know where they were going. I got lucky with one scoop and forked a large ball of them over the side. I wonder if they bounced when they hit the ground far below.

Finally, I said goodbye to the last one, and took a closer look at the skeleton before me. Sitting upright against that wall, the old boy's ribs had been a climbing trellis for those snakes, long before the first white man came this way. The remnants of a robe were turning to dust on him. Whoever he had been, he never left his post. I had heard the Indians talk of "The Old Ones" who came before. I thought they were legends.

I explored the hallway heading into the butte and shortly found myself on top of the world. Able to see all directions, I focused on a dust trail a few miles away from me, headed away from me to the south. I could only make out a couple of horses, but couldn't tell if they were ridden or not. I turned back into the downward passage, still alert for rattlers, and investigated the other two passages.

The first one led to another landing, such as the first one I had found, with one difference. It had a drain carved into the rock, which would funnel the scarce rainwater from the rock floor to a stone culvert below. It held some now.

The second passageway led down for only a short distance, to a storage room. The rock ledges carved in the room's walls were lined with pottery of different sizes and markings unfamiliar to me. Feeling illiterate, I started to examine the jugs contents, and expected to find some old grain or seeds. Instead, I grabbed handfuls of; quartz, turquoise, and some other stones I couldn't identify, but had a unique look to them. They were rare or special in some way. I reached the bottom row of large jugs that lined the room, and stuck my hand inside it. I touched the contents, and immediately knew what it was without seeing it. I pulled out a handful of gold nuggets similar to the one I had found. My fist didn't want to release its prize where I could see it.

"I must have died and gone to heaven!" I said aloud. That bunch of bones up there must be King Solomon himself. If all those jugs contain gold, there might be over a hundred million dollars here! I felt dizzy. I filled every pocket I had in my pants and coat, and then my hat. I went outside to sit and catch my breath. I pinched myself to make sure I was awake.

I sat on a stone bench with the cool breeze blowing in my face, and my breathing got back to normal. I looked at King Solomon, wondering if he knew how big a fortune he had guarded for centuries. In his day, it was probably just a bunch of pretty stones, used for barter and making jewelry. Now, it was something that men would kill for.

One way I can pay back my good fortune, is to give the king a proper burial. It would have to be down below. There was no place to dig here. Unceremoniously, I picked up all of his bones and skull, and pitched them over the side. I knew they would land close to each other, and I could bury them right there.

I climbed down the stairs carefully, not wanting to fall to the rocks below, and become the next guardian of this desert castle. I reached the bottom and loaded the gold out of my hat and pockets into my saddlebags. I felt like I was going to float away, I weighed so much less.

I spent the next few hours piling stones in front of those stairs, as high as I could reach, and filled the gaps with sandy dirt. When I was finished, you couldn't tell where it had been if you didn't already know. I was glad I spared the cactus and hadn't beat them down. I very gently pulled each one back to the previous cover it provided.

I looked for the old king's bones where I thought I had dropped them over the side of the butte, but they weren't on the ground below. They must have caught in the rocks on the way down. At least I had good intentions. I pointed my horse west and headed towards home.

* * *

Aieee!! I have done the spirit dance all morning, seeking forgiveness from the mountain Ganh. I thought it unwise to come back, but Stone Knife taunted me and Pony Stealer had laughed with him. Together we came back to face the Ganh against my advice. Stone Knife then angered the Ganh saying disrespectful things about the Ganh and that he wasn't afraid of him. I told him this would anger Him and it did!

The Ganh caused it to rain rattlesnakes on his head, finally hitting him with many tied in a knot, knocking him off his horse. No longer disbelievers and screaming like young squaws, he and Pony Stealer galloped their horses away fast, and never looked back.

One has to atone for the disrespect shown by of the others in his tribe, and I stayed to do the spirit dance to appease the Ganh. As I finished, I swore on the bones of my father, to always honor this Ganh, in whatever appearance He assumes. I caught a glimpse of Him in the rocks in the shape of the soldier with the gray coat. I closed my eyes, silently finishing my promise, and something rained down around me. Fearing it was rattlesnakes I quickly opened my eyes and it was...Father!

I gathered his bones for my mother, and rode away. I knew the Ganh made it so, and I would honor my promise. Mother said I was meant to be a holy man, now she will be proud that her son Turtle serves the Ganh. I shall now be called Turtle the Wise.

Chapter 4

I had plenty of time to study on things on the rest of my trip home. I had enough gold in my saddle bags to do anything I'd ever imagined, but dreaming and doing are different things. It was also enough money to get my throat cut and my body buried in a shallow grave. I kept my eyes open wide and my head on a swivel.

In the distance, I saw a dust storm coming, and looked for a gully or arroyo to take cover in. The storm wasn't getting any bigger as it moved towards me, and there was something familiar about that cloud of dust.

I led the buckskin to the shade of a rock outcropping, and squinted at the dust cloud until it was close enough to see it wasn't a storm, but a sea of cattle. I saw several riders keeping the herd bunched and moving, and some distance back were the chuck and supply wagons. As they came near, I saw the riders more distinctly, and it was obvious who the owner and trail boss were from their actions. One rider kept to the rear of the herd and watched everything, with an occasional look back him at the two wagons straggling behind. Seeing the concern and attentiveness he displayed, I figured he was the owner, or a damned good trail boss. Ramrods are always moving, and riders sort of keep their place on the outside of a herd.

As the herd drew even with me, a tall lanky outrider peeled away and rode in my direction. Hands on a cattle drive don't cotton to a stranger watching their herd. I met him with a smile and my hands on the saddle pommel, away from my guns.

"Howdy, looks like you boys been on a steady diet of dust," I said.

He looked over the remains of my worn out uniform and said, "Reb, you don't know the half of it. If I were to take a bath I'd lose fifteen pounds of Texas. I'm surprised the sheriff ain't arrested me for landgrabbing."

I held out my hand and said, "Jack Shane, headed home to New Mexico from the war. I've been a long time gone. Who does this mountain of beef belong to?

He reached for my hand with his, and said, "Call me Rooster, the herd belongs to C.W. Motes from down big bend way. We are driving the herd to the Midland stockyards, and I got plans to stir up the local saloon economy as soon as they are sold." He laughed with his head bobbing up and down, and you could see why they called him Rooster. He had a laugh that spread all over you, and had you laughing with him. Before you knew it, your head was bobbing too.

I rode along with him on the outskirts of the herd, to help keep the herd bunched and enjoying the cows and company. The trail boss called a halt to the drive at a small stream to allow the cows to drink their fill. Water was scarce this far south, and it was best to drink anytime it was available.

Rooster said, "You had me worried when I first saw you in that uniform. I thought you might be one of them renegades we been hearing about. When the war was over, a lot of jail doors swung open that shouldn't have, and they let some jokers out who were better left on the other side of that door. Most of them were deserters or just plain bad. The kind of men who used the war to cover their crimes. While they don't want to earn an honest day's pay, they sure do work hard trying to steal what little money honest folks have."

I accepted an invite to the chuck for beef and beans. It was a feast compared to my usual fair. On a drive, the trail cook was an important part of the crew. A good one had the cowboys looking forward to putting on their food bags at night and in good spirits around the campfires afterward. A bad one could get shot. This one had a mighty fair hand with a cook stove. He spiced up the beef and beans with some peppers and onions which got the plates licked clean.

You could see this was a good trail crew, tightly put together and led by a man they all respected. A cowboy will work for wages, but if he respects you then he'll ride through hell for your brand.

After supper, I asked C.W. if he had time to step aside with me and talk a little business. He said, "Always." I asked him what price he expected to get in Midland for the herd, and how many head he approximated he had right now. As I knew he would, he told me the numbers off the top of his head and how much money he expected to make off the transaction. There were over twelve hundred head plus a few calves.

I asked him, "Would you drive them north up the Pecos for another five dollars a head?"

Just like that we had a deal. He told me jokingly if it was going to be in Confederate script the price would be a lot higher. In private, I pulled out my food sack with half the gold in it and told him, "This should cover the price of the cows, the crew's time, and a drinking bonus."

He looked at it, then back at me, and said, "By damn, I believe it will!"

For the next few days, because of the rank displayed on my old uniform, I was now, "Captain Jack" to the riders. I got to know them all. Most of them were good old boys and a lot of them were just boys, some on their first drive. They wouldn't be boys by the time they got home with this drive under their belt, along with a saloon or two, and maybe a sporting house. They would have tales to tell when they returned home.

Rooster had a tale or two to tell every night at the campfire, and he would take a few liberties with the stories, making them more "listenable" as he put it. When he got to the end of a tale his head would start bobbing, and his infectious laugh would come galloping out of his mouth. It would have the other hands laughing and bobbing their heads too. I was going to miss this when it came time to leave this bunch. I couldn't remember this much laughter, and enjoying the company of a friendly bunch of men since early in the war years.

Since I didn't sleep too well anyway, I helped the out riders on the night rounds keep the herd quiet and predators away. I heard Rooster in the darkness singing to the cattle, to let them know he was near.

"Have a shot of good whiskey and I'll do the same,
Then let's pour another and do it again.
Let's talk of old places, let's talk of old friends,
Remember old faces and old times again."

It was time for me to ride ahead to the ranch. There were preparations to make to receive the herd, and I was unsure of what awaited me there, I had been away a long time. I had mailed a letter home at war's end, but the territorial mail was unreliable, even before the war. The next morning, after a cup of Pappy Smith's black coffee and some sourdough biscuits with molasses, I shook hands with the crew, and regretted having to part company with them. I headed north towards home with reminders from Rooster and C. W., to watch for renegades and Indians. Waving goodbye, I patted my long gun and checked my pistol loads.

Chapter 5

I was riding into higher country now as I neared home, and I fit into this land like an oiled gun in a new leather holster. This country and I liked each other considerably. It was hard to believe the desert and these high valleys were created at the same time. The hot and flat plains below must have been made first, before this garden of Eden in the high country.

The water was sweeter and the grass taller. I have never seen anything as beautiful in all my travels. The yucca and sotol cactus were blooming, standing like sentinels alongside the yellow roses on the prickly pear, and the red blooms on the long thorny ocotillo branches.

If you haven't witnessed spring time in this part of New Mexico, I'm sorry for you, because I don't have the words to do it justice describing it. The tall green grass blows in the wind, and makes you want to lie down in it and count the clouds. The trees had greened out in defiance of the winter past, and it all made you feel good to be alive and part of it.

A slight odor of smoke in the air turned my attention from the enjoyment of the day. I saw a wisp of it at the other end of the valley, maybe a half mile away. Smoke means fire, and fire means people or lightning. There hadn't been a storm so it had to be people. The presence of people can mean anything from a shared cup of coffee over a campfire, to a cabin burnt out by Indians. I trotted my horse toward the smoke.

The valley curved, following the river that had formed it, and I could hear gunshots as I rounded the bend. I didn't think I'd be sharing a cup of coffee. I slipped my long gun out of the scabbard and galloped to the fray.

I heard handguns popping, and blasts from a shotgun that quieted the guns momentarily. When I rounded the bend of the river, I saw a box wagon and team of horses stuck in the mud of the riverbed. A woman wearing a blue calico dress was proving everything I had ever heard about red heads true.

She was inside the wagon firing a stage gun over the wagon's tailgate. A half dozen men fired pistols at her, and were trying to push a burning wagon toward hers. She tried to shoot under the wagon, but didn't have a good enough angle to cause them grief.

I decided to even the odds against the cowards who would try to burn a woman out of her wagon. I swung through the woods behind them and charged. I fired my Henry as fast as I could lever shells into the chamber. My reward was a yelp of pain, and the rabble scattered into the woods. Wishing I had my saber, I pursued and they fled like the cowards they were. I noticed they wore both gray and blue uniforms. These must be the renegades I had been warned about. One of them had a shock of white hair belying his age, and it stirred a memory, but I couldn't place him at the moment.

I emptied one of my pistols at them to make sure they didn't turn around. If they knew I was alone, they might have tried to make a fight of it. And I wished they would. I reloaded my Colt and Henry rifle before I turned to the wagon.

I was met with the stage gun pointed at me, and the look in that red headed woman's bright green eyes...well, I was glad I was on her side. I hoped she knew it.

"Easy now, lady," I said as gently as I could, "it takes a while to slow yourself back down after something like this. My name is Jack Shane, and I'm a rancher in this area returning home from the war. You can see I'm on your side. Please lower that gun, ma'am. I got no wish to look like a salt shaker."

She lowered the barrel. I started breathing again.

"My husband and I were overtaken by that bunch. We tried to get away, but got stuck in the riverbed sand," she said.

"Where is your husband ma'am?" I asked. Then I heard a groan from inside the wagon which answered my question.

I dropped the tailgate, and saw a sight I had seen too many times in the war. A man lay there gut shot, and in a lot of pain. I asked the missus to get some rags and clean water ready, and I fetched a jug of bourbon out of my saddlebags. If this wasn't medicinal purposes, nothing was. I gave him a pull on the jug then took one myself. I nodded to the woman and then the bottle, but she shook her head.

I took her rags and the whiskey jug, and went to work on him. I cut the shirt off the wounded area, and rinsed the skin clean with whiskey. I tied a wad of clean rags to the wound as tight as I could get it. Depending on how much damage the bullet had torn up inside, he might have a chance if he didn't lose any more blood, but not a very good one. I'd rather bet on a pair of deuces.

I hitched my buckskin in tandem with the wagon team. While the woman stood watch with the shotgun, I pulled the wagon along with the horses. Slowly, the wheels climbed out of the sand to harder ground. When we stopped, I checked the running gear and it appeared not to have suffered any damage.

We could journey to my ranch by tomorrow night, so I offered, and she accepted my hospitality. I hoped the trip wouldn't kill her husband. We couldn't remain here with those renegades in the area. They might get braver after dark. I tied my horse to the back of the wagon, and took the team's reins while the woman tended to her husband.

Before dark, I pulled the wagon into a small clearing where I had camped before. There was good water nearby, shelter from the wind, and cover enough for a small campfire. I unhitched the team, and staked them in some tall grass with water close by.

I rode about a mile down our back trail, and as expected, saw no signs of pursuit. The odds had changed for that pond scum with me in the picture, and as far as they knew, maybe even more guns. Those men were cowards with no stomach for a fight they might not win. They would look for easier pickings elsewhere.

Returning to camp I smelled supper cooking, and it reminded me I hadn't eaten all day. I looked in the back of the wagon to check on the wounded man. The wound had stopped bleeding, and he was out like a light. I had left the jug of bourbon with him, and he was smart enough to drink it.

I tended to my buckskin and the wagon team. My horse seemed grateful for the company of the others. The familiar smell of coffee was in the air. I turned to the fire where a coffeepot sat. I picked it up and poured some in a tin cup placed next to the campfire. I sat on the ground cross legged enjoying the coffee, and wished the jug of bourbon was handy.

The woman was cooking some stew on a camp stove over the fire. She ladled some into a bowl and handed it to me. I nodded my thanks. She peered in the wagon checking on her husband, then dipped herself a bowl. She sat on the ground next to me. Neither of us talked or ate with much appetite, but the necessities of survival such as nourishment have to be observed. There would be plenty of time for talking tomorrow. It was very tasty stew, but the earlier events had brought back a lot of memories best left in the past. She was still in a combat trance I had seen many times after the young'un's first firefights during the war. Thanking her for the stew, I checked on the horses, then unrolled my bedroll under the wagon. I placed my long gun next to me, pulled up my blanket, and went to sleep.

I saw them coming up the hill in the dark, and tried to warn the rest of the company, but it was too late. We were being overrun. Where was our sentry? Was he dead? Men were charging and firing as they came. They had their bayonets stabbing, and slashing sleeping men and I...!

"Wake up Mr. Shane! Wake up! It's all right!"

Someone was pulling at my boot. From the terror in my mind I wandered through the fog of sleep to the time and place I was supposed to be. My heart was racing and I was soaked with sweat. Mumbling my apologies over and over, I felt like a fool. I crawled out from under the wagon. The woman was there in her nightgown with the shotgun in the crook of her arm. I wanted to laugh, but was afraid it might not come out sounding as a laugh.

She said, "You woke me yelling, 'they're coming, they're coming!' I grabbed the shotgun, and got out of the wagon looking for those renegades coming to bring us more grief. Instead, I find you in a nightmare I hope I never have mister."

There was nothing I could say. She said goodnight, and returned to her bed in the wagon. I pulled my bedroll out from under the wagon, and rolled it up.

It was going to be a few hours until daylight, but I needed some coffee and didn't want to disturb them anymore this night. I built up the fire, and made coffee. I sat back from the fire to keep my night vision, and listened to the sounds of the night until dawn.

Chapter 6

Every turn of the wagon wheels brought us closer to the ranch. By noon, we had traveled several miles. The wounded man in the back of the wagon had regained consciousness, and listening to his groans, I knew his wound conveyed every bump in the road.

I scouted the trail both ahead and behind, but saw nothing of interest. I tied my horse to the wagon, climbed into the seat, and took the reins. The woman nodded her thanks. She stepped back into the wagon bed to check on her husband. I heard her sobbing softly. Teary eyed, she returned with her lips tight and jaw set firmly.

She sat down beside me and said, "I may have traveled a long way to become a widow. We lost everything when the Union Troops came through Georgia burning everything in their path. They even killed the livestock they didn't steal. We tried to rebuild, but the carpetbaggers showed up on the doorstep one day with papers giving them our land, because they could pay the taxes on it and we couldn't." Her lips pulled tight as those green eyes stared blankly into the past. She wanted to talk so I sat and listened.

"It broke Jim. The land had been in the Sullivan family since the thirties. All the scoundrels wanted it for was to parcel it off at a profit. The only people to ever live on it besides the Sullivans were Indians. We put together what we had left for this trip." Her face relaxed and there was the start of a smile on it.

"The old Jim was starting to come back with each mile we put behind us. We planned a new start in California, and if he lives, we may still have a chance to get there." She sat there in silence for a moment, then turned to me as if she had remembered something.

"Sorry, but I'm still fighting yesterday's battle in my head. My name is Kathleen Sullivan and my husband's is James. Please call me Kate, and him Jim, we are just plain folks and comfortable being so."

I extended my right hand, and said, "Pleased to meet you, Mrs. Kate Sullivan. When you were holding a shotgun on me I told you my name was Jack, but you were strung tighter than a banjo string at the time. I'm the owner of the Shane ranch, or at least I was before the war. It was free and clear before the war, and I don't think the carpetbaggers have made it this far west. The ranch is big in area, but not much else, some cattle, and a few sheep. There is a Mexican family and my niece living there. Guess you can tell from my clothes where I've been."

She glance at me and smiled.

"No Missus Shane waiting for you?"

My mind traveled to a small graveyard beneath tall cottonwoods, close to my ranch house. I felt something turn over in my chest.

"Yes 'ma'am, in a way she is."

She hesitated a moment, then faced me, obviously curious at my choice of words. Her red hair fell from her bonnet when she turned, and the wind blew it across her face. I was reminded of the streaks the sun painted the sky with as it was setting. She twisted the errant locks, tucking them in place, and I could see the question in her eyes before she asked it.

"I don't understand," she said.

"She is buried on the ranch with my sister, Anne. She

miscarried, and died of hemorrhaging, a couple of years before the war started."

She looked genuinely saddened at my loss.

"I'm so sorry. And your sister?"

"They said it was pneumonia, but if you can die of a broken heart, then that's the real cause. My brother-in-law was killed by Comanches on a raiding party that passed through the area stealing horses and taking scalps. He got Anne and Charley to safety, but at the cost of his life. She wasted away after that, and went downhill until pneumonia took her."

"Life must be hard out here."

Six years ago I had held my wife's cold hand, and watched the light go out of her and me too. I thought of a little girl wearing a linsey-woolsey dress, her arms spread across her mother's grave, and crying her eyes out.

"Sometimes it is," I answered.

We talked for several hours, and I enjoyed being in the company of a female, which hadn't been often since Meg died. It was a comforting reminder there was still some gentleness in the world. She asked a lot of questions about the ranch and area I was glad to answer. I looked forward to her spending time with Charley, however long it might be. The only women she had contact with were: Consuelo at the ranch and the seldom visit from distant neighbors.

The sun had slid behind the horizon. Twilight was falling when I saw a light in the direction of the ranch. I asked Kate to stay with the wagon, while I made sure all was well at home. Familiar things were everywhere now, and weight was lifting from my shoulders.

I rode up to the small fenced plot under the cottonwoods next to the water. The graves had been tended, and as a tear rolled down my face I said, "I'm home, Meg." I dismounted and bent down to kiss the top of the marker. After a moment, I mounted my horse and rode to the lantern light at the corner of the house.

When I approached, a woman walked out on the dog run, rifle in hand, squinting at me in the twilight shadows. A familiar voice said, "Is that you Unka Jack?"

"It's me, but where is Charley, and who are you sounding like her?"

With a happy giggle, she launched herself off the porch, and said, "It's me, come down here off that horse and give me a hug. I thought you might be some varmint that needed shooting when I saw you riding in, but when you went down by the cottonwoods, I knowed it had to be you."

I stepped off my horse, intending to scoop her up as I always had, but she didn't fit my scoop anymore. I still had her in my mind as a child, barely in her teens. My mind had a lot of catching up to do. There were a lot of women her age already married and making young'uns. This would take some getting used to. I told her about the Sullivans and she made ready for them while I went to bring them in.

We got Jim into the house, and in the bed. He looked ragged. From the sweat beaded up on his forehead, I knew it was a painful trip from the wagon. The wound had stopped bleeding. A good sign.

Charley was already bending Kate's ear asking how she could help. I left them and walked the short distance to the Mancha's house. Juan saw me coming and ran to meet me, *"Patrono que han venido a casa! Consuelo!* Slapping me on the back, he dragged me to the house for hugs from Consuelo and little Juan. Consuelo pulled me to the table, with no resistance from me. They must have been eating supper because there was food already on the table. Tortillas, beans and rice, and always the peppers. I had missed this. It was great to be home. I told her of our guests, and immediately there was a great clatter of pots and pans out in the kitchen. Soon she and little Juan ran out the door carrying supper for the others. I was with family

22

again.

Juan and I sat drinking coffee and talking. I found out there had been little change since I had left. The war had bypassed our valley. I thanked him and Consuelo for all they had done for Charley and the ranch in my absence. He waved it off. We were all family, and they loved Charley and the ranch as much as I did.

I told him of the herd coming our way, and we made plans to receive them. We discussed the preparations we must make with no mention of how they had been acquired. It was merely accepted there had been good fortune.

After a while, I walked back to the main house. I unrolled my bedroll outside on the dog run, where at least I had a roof over my head. I had been sleeping outside for a long time, and had no problem giving up my bed to Charley and Kate. I slept soundly until dawn, my only dreams of green grass and home.

Chapter 7

The ringing of my hammer blows upon the anvil echoed across the valley. I forged our new brand out of iron bar stock. Charley pumped the bellows for me until the iron stock was white hot, and easily formed in a V. After making three of them, I welded them to a rod where they formed the branding iron symbol, >>> for the new brand and name we had given our ranch, Three Arrows.

Charley wore the necklace she had made out of the three arrowheads I had given her. I told her of my encounter with the Indians with no mention of the gold of course.

"Unka Jack," she said, and held the arrowheads up to me, "look close at them, they are shaped like little turtles."

I held them up and she was right. There were five small barbs where a turtle's head and legs would have been. Those barbs were the reason I had to cut the arrowhead out of my chest. The Apache who made those arrowheads was a craftsman alright. A warrior too, from the damage his arrows could do.

We worked from dawn to dusk preparing for the herd's pending arrival. Juan and I recruited help from the closest ranches to assist. We built pens and gates, and fenced off most of the rough country. We needed to raise another barn along with a dozen other projects.

Jim Sullivan was holding his own. I upped the bet in my head on whether or not he would make it to a pair of tens. I hoped he would ante up jacks or better. Charley and I were going to miss Kate when she left the ranch. Her presence added something we had missed since Meg had passed. She left a glow throughout the house and kitchen. Her cooking made me anticipate every meal, and my ribs had started to disappear.

I would make a bank deposit my first trip to town. The last thing I wanted to do was draw attention to the gold itself. Cows don't shine as much as gold does. I studied on all that gold at the butte too. That much money could do a lot of good or bad in the wrong hands. There were some fanatics out there who, with that kind of financing, could possibly start the war back up.

"*Patron!* The *vacas!* Little Juan has seen them from the top of the cliff," yelled an excited, Juan. This was going to be a good day.

I yelled, "Come along *amigo*, we have work to do." I saddled my horse and we rode down the valley to meet C. W. Motes and our cows.

When we stopped at a small rise, Juan's eyes got big as saucers, and he talked so fast in Spanish I started laughing. He grinned.

"*Patron*, I have never seen so many cattles. As far as I can see, they just keep moving this way. We need some more riders *pronto!*" I had been thinking the same thing. We rode down to meet the herd. A familiar face and laugh met us halfway there.

Juan said, "Theese must be *El Gallo, Si?*"

"Yeah," I grinned at both of them, "but I think he answers better to Rooster."

We shook hands all around, and rode with the other riders steering the herd down the valley. In a couple of hours, we had driven the herd to the far end of the valley where the green grass would keep them bunched. We would separate them later for branding and breeding. I see many a long day in our future.

Returning to the ranch house, I saw the chuck had rolled up next to the kitchen and smoke coming out the chimney. Some of it blew my way, and I knew there were going to be a lot of happy cowboys tonight. Consuelo, and Pappy Smith would be in competition to see who could fire up the hottest supper. There were probably enough hot peppers in the food to cook it without a fire. *Caliente!* Just the way I liked it.

In anticipation of the feast to come, the boys washed the trail dust off and brushed their clothes. Some of them even put on a clean shirt. Several of us sat in the shade of the ranch house ramada smoking cigars and drinking brandy, courtesy of C. W. The usual subjects of cows and weather were kicked around and Rooster told a couple of tales which got us all to laughing and heads bobbing.

I made an open offer for cowhands, to any of them who wanted stick for a while. I had already paid for their whiskey bonus, along with a few days in Midland saloons and sporting houses, and that was occupying most of their minds. I asked them to think on it while they were here. I let them know there was a bunk and a place at the table here for them after Midland, if they wanted to light here a spell. The gate was open.

C. W. filled my cup with some more brandy, and said, "It's a pleasure doing business with you, Captain Jack. Most buyers take ownership of that herd, and send us on our way, eager to be shut of us cowboys. You have invited us into your home, welcomed us to your table, and treated us like family. That means a lot to old cowboys like me and Rooster. Ain't many this hospitable. You know how it is on the trail, you never get enough sleep, or even sit down in a chair after a long day in the saddle. You seldom get to wash the dust off, and too tired to do so when you do have water available. On top of that, you paid a better than fair price."

I was afraid he was going to mention the gold, but he knew to be cautious where money was concerned.

"One thing I feel I better pass on to you," he continued, "those renegades we talked about were dogging our trail. The reason I know it was renegades, and not Apaches, is because we saw them. Wouldn't have seen the Indians."

He paced the ramada and stepped down to the ground walking in front of my chair. I could see concern in his face. His next words brought a chill down my spine.

"Vass Hart is the leader of the gang!"

Chapter 8

Vass Hart! A man who needed killing a long time ago, and some fool sent him to prison instead of a firing squad. That fool was me. White hair on a man running through the pines. Now I know why it looked familiar. There were men who didn't return home from the war because of him. Hart was assigned sentry duty the night our company was overrun by Union troops. Men were killed in the surprise attack, some still in their bedrolls. There was no warning because his sentry post was abandoned. He was captured the next day, asleep in a millinery shop in town. Apparently, he planned to rob the owner who opened the shop early, and found him sleeping. The owner summoned the sheriff and Hart was arrested without a fight.

I was the presiding officer at his court martial. I sentenced him to life in a military prison instead of the firing squad he deserved. He never opened his mouth in defense of his absence and dereliction of duty. He was hiding something he feared worse than a firing squad. He had probably been released when the war ended since his crime occurred when he had was in the Confederate army. I had a feeling we would be getting reacquainted soon. I felt my jaw tighten.

C. W. gave me a queer look. "From that look on your face, you must have crossed paths with that butt nugget somewhere. I'm glad I'm not him."

"Back during the war he needed killing, and I didn't

accommodate him," I said. I related to him what had happened during the war, including my feelings at the time.

C.W. took a sip from his glass and a slow draw on his cigar before he spoke, "Sometimes it's better to let a man off, than to string him up. I caught a good boy roping one of my cows a few months ago. He had to feed his mother and sister. He came home from the war to a starving family and buried father. There wasn't much of their stock or ranch left, after a fire started by some northern sympathizers burned the barn and house down. Now I had every right to string him up, but he weren't no outlaw. I took him home with that steer, and made arrangements to move his mother and sister to my ranch in a few days. I signed him on as a cowhand, with the understanding that cow would come out of his wages. He showed up with; a horse, his gear, and Sharps fifty caliber with a shooter's scope on it. This boy was a sharpshooter in the war, and he put a lot of men under. I can vouch for his shooting. You wouldn't want him coming after you, but he's not a killer. If it meets with your approval, Captain, I'm going to ask him to stay a spell with you until this renegade trouble blows away. His name is Cort Benner."

I remembered the boy from the time I spent with the herd. Good looking kid with a sad, serious, look about him. He was friendly though, and a hard worker. I hadn't noticed his rifle, he probably had it stored in one of the wagons. He would be a welcome addition as a hand, as well as his sharpshooting.

Supper was as good as expected. I think Pappy Smith would have married Consuelo on the spot, if Juan would have let him. She was showing him how to use dried peppers from the *ristra* hanging by the cook fire, and how to make *chili verde* with *tomatillos* and *cilantro*. She already had him a box of spices and garden vegetables packed for the journey south.

The pitchers of water and tea were passed often to wide eyed cowboys, with beads of sweat dripping off their nose from eating the hot peppers. Juan and a couple of the hands played their guitars and sang songs with bawdy lyrics, as attested to the looks Consuelo gave him, and the snickers from the cowboys who understood Spanish.

The Sullivans sat in the kitchen with Charley. They weren't being unsociable. Jim was healing, but wasn't up to the occasion, and Charley had become Kathleen's caboose. I was having a good time with good people. It would be the last time for one of them.

The next morning, we sat outside drinking coffee and watching the sun rise over the valley ridge. The smells from the kitchen cooking fires stirred my appetite. Looking at the cowboys sitting around me, I wasn't the only one.

Rooster approached me and said, "Me and a few of the boys want to know if that offer for hands is still open. I wouldn't mind hanging around for a spell. Too many years of sleeping in the saddle and on hard ground has made my old bones feel older. No offense to Pappy Smith, but the cooking is a sight better here too."

I smiled at my good fortune. These men were sorely needed at the ranch with the arrival of the herd. I said, "You all got a job."

Two of the cowboys were Lonnie and Ben Butterfield, brothers from the Texas panhandle. I asked them why a couple of young bucks like them wanted to get tied down as ranch hands. Lonnie had a bad stutter, but he and Ben joked about it and put us all at ease.

"L-L-L-onnie st-st-stutters sometimes," said Ben.

"I'm gonna k-k-k-...," Lonnie said.

"Kick," Ben laughed.

"Y-y-your butt," Lonnie finished.

"Captain Jack, we want to see the country, and we already seen Texas all the way to the border. We figure we could stay on for a few months, and get to see a lot of new ground right here.

By then, we'll be getting itchy feet, and you'll have hired more hands."

We spent the day fencing the only exit from the end of the valley where the cattle did the majority of their grazing. The trail crew helped and the fence was up by late afternoon. I appreciated the help considering the fact most cowboys don't like to work out of the saddle unless they have to. I would make sure they were well fed again tonight.

"I-I-Indian!" Lonnie said from behind me. "In the r-r-rocks!"

I made a quick turn in the saddle but saw nothing. Maybe it had been an Indian or maybe an animal. If it were an Indian, he was traveling, and the ranch happened to be in his path. Still, I would keep my eyes open.

The next morning, Rooster, Cort, and myself rode south for a few miles with the trail crew as they left for Midland and a bonus spending spree. We looked for strays along the way. Some had wandered when the herd was being driven to the valley entrance. We rounded a few of them up and started them toward the main herd. We said goodbye to C. W. and the crew, and they promised to drink one for us when they reached Midland. I had no doubt they would keep their promises.

It was past noon, when we neared the ranch house. The Butterfield brothers took charge of the strays, and guided them down the valley. Rooster, Cort, and I rode to the house, they hadn't met Charley or the Sullivans yet. When we got there, I saw a strange wagon tied up to our hitching rail. We had a visitor.

A little fat man with a small trunk was sitting on the ramada, next to a dance hall girl that looked a lot like my niece, Charley, standing on the dog run. She met Cort's wide eyed stare with one of her own, and walked off the porch. She landed face down in the dirt. Cort didn't do much better. The lantern post caught him under the chin, and set him on the ground with a thud. They both jumped off the ground, and ran to each other, shouting in unison, "Are you alright?" They dusted themselves off, then stood looking each other in the eye.

Now I've heard of love at first sight, and even seen chickens mesmerized, but nothing held a candle to this. I wasn't sure I liked the attention Charley was getting from, and worse, was returning to, Cort. Kathleen, came out of the house and smiled. I don't know if it was at the two of them or my discomfort. Or both.

I yelled, "Charley! What is that you are wearing?"

She turned her gaze my way, still entranced. She had a look in her eyes like she had been struck by lightning. Kate patted her on the shoulder and went back inside.

The little fat man stood up, offered me his hand, and said, "Sir, if I may, my name is Maxie, and I sold that fine garment to your daughter. Another customer wanted it, but I saved it for this young lady. I am employed by a lady's wear company back east, and I am seeking new sales territories here in the west. I am sure she will be fine momentarily, when the shock of youth wears off."

"My niece," I corrected. "Kathleen, would you help her? Please."

She stepped out the door chuckling, and nudged Charley into the kitchen. Cort, meanwhile, continued to stare into space.

Rooster, laughed. He grabbed Cort by his belt and said, "Come on Romeo."

Chapter 9

We were eating supper when we heard gunshots. I rose from the table, as did Rooster and Cort, and headed for the door. The Butterfield brothers were riding toward the house hell bent for leather with pistols in hand.

"Whoa, boys! Have we got trouble, or are you that hungry?" I said.

"Those renegades are after our cows! Lonnie took a shot at them from a distance to stop them from cutting some cattle out to rustle, and they are right behind us!"

"How many?" I asked.

"I counted eight, but there may be a couple more."

"T-t-there was one with w-w-white hair," added Lonnie.

"How much time do we have before they get here?" I asked.

"A couple of minutes, they were a distance from us and spread out."

I ran for the house with an idea in my head that would even the odds some if it worked. I grabbed my gray greatcoat and hat, off of the wall hooks, and yelled at Charley to bring me the sack of rock salt. I grabbed the stage gun off the gun rack, and flew out the door. I ran to the lantern post in the center of the courtyard, and put the greatcoat around the lantern arms and the hat on top of the post. I tied the shotgun to the post, midways down its length. Charley, met me with the rock salt, and I packed both barrels full on top of the powder loads. I tied a loop of cord around the two triggers, and cocked the hammers. I unrolled the ball of cord while walking backwards to the barn door.

Rooster and Cort strung a rope across the entrance to the courtyard, about a foot off the ground. This was going to be interesting.

The lanterns were hung behind the lantern post, which accented the outline of the hat and coat. The figure posed a distraction I hoped would give us the edge. We barely had time to take cover when we saw them coming at a full gallop. I stepped inside the barn door with the cord in my hand. The other men hid in the shadows.

The renegades, being war veterans probably figured numbers and surprise would be sufficient to charge in here and take us down. Unfortunately for them, I had a little experience in tactics too.

They rode hard out of the dark, and fired at the lantern post figure as they charged. A white haired rider led the way. His horse was the first to go down. The horses' legs hit the rope, sending the outlaws flying over their heads to land heavily on the ground. Men and horses rolled a few yards in front of the post figure they had been shooting at. It was mass confusion. The renegades were trying to get to their feet when I pulled the cord on the shotgun triggers, giving them both barrels of rock salt. They screamed out in pain, and rubbed their stinging skin and eyes burned with rock salt. Horses were bucking and letting it known they didn't cotton to being treated this way. Most of the fight had gone out of the men, at this point but it wasn't over yet. Charley ran out on the porch holding a pistol with both hands, and firing as fast as she could pull the trigger. The first shot hit the barn door above my head and I dove in the barn. The next two bullets took out the weather vane, and slammed into the chicken house adding to the commotion. The remainder of the shots ricocheted around the yard. Everyone hugged the ground.

A voice yelled, "We give up, we give up, stop shooting!" It was Rooster.

Vass Hart rose to his feet. Seeing Charley standing there with an empty pistol, he drew his knife and ran for her. A dark figure leaped off the porch like a panther. Jim Sullivan drove a shoulder into him, taking him off his feet and laying him out cold when he hit the ground. Jim fell to his knees next to him with his head hanging down. Saving Charley had cost him dearly. He had taken the knife meant for her.

Cort Benner pulled the hammer back on his handgun and stuck it against a head of white hair. I didn't like the look in his eyes.

"Easy son, she's alright and he's got worse coming if you don't drop that hammer," I said. It was a hard thing for him, and I'm not sure I didn't want him to pull the trigger.

He made the right choice. He uncocked the hammer and holstered his weapon. We tied them up and locked them in the log smokehouse. They weren't going anywhere. We tethered their horses and gathered some coils of rope from the barn. The renegades were going to regret this attack in the morning.

Before dawn, we lifted all the riders into their saddles except for Hart. I had other plans for him. We led them down the valley to a large oak tree by the river. It had eight ropes tied in nooses hanging from it. One for each rider. We placed the nooses over their heads and tightened them. One man prayed and a couple pled for their lives. The rest were silent. I told them to make their peace, and some of the younger ones started to cry. I nodded, we fired our guns in the air, and eight men were yanked out of the saddle. They landed on their butts in the dirt. I had tied all the ropes longer than hanging length. I had seen enough death the last four years.

We removed the ropes while each man coughed and rubbed his throat. We helped them to their feet. I pointed the barrel of my Colt in each one's face and said, "This is the second and last chance you will ever get from this ranch. You all have two choices I promise to make happen for you. You can ride out of here as soon as you find your horse, and a shorter rope will be waiting should you ever return."

"What's the other choice?" a raspy young voice asked.

"My name is Captain Jack Shane. This is the Three Arrows ranch. Anyone of you who will ride for the brand, and give me an honest day's work will get a square deal here. You have my word on that. You can throw a rope here, or hang from it boys. Your choice. Consuelo will have breakfast on the table, by the time you catch your horses and get back to the ranch, if you decide to stay."

None of them asked about Vass Hart.

Chapter 10

We added six more cowhands that morning. The two hardest looking outlaws, Rafe Hall and Cliff Britt, chose to leave. They wouldn't get another chance at Three Arrows. Some men would rather gamble on a rope than do a hard day's work. Sooner or later, the rope would win the last hand in that game.

Jim Sullivan's face was a gray pallor when I went to the house to check on his condition. Kathleen had been at his side throughout the night, and I offered to spell her so she could rest. She didn't want to leave his side, but she had to sleep sometime. I figured she was thinking this was time she may never get back. I promised to wake her if anything changed. Five minutes later, she was asleep on Charley's bed.

I was sitting there drinking coffee when Jim woke up.

He looked at me and said, "Kate?"

"Asleep," I answered. He nodded as if to say that was good.

"Jack, can I ask you for a promise?" His eyes had a question in them.

"The answer is yes if it's what I think it is. I owe you more than can be repaid, Jim."

"If you're talking about what happened with Charley last night, you don't owe me a thing. I wish I'd had that stage gun loaded with buckshot so I could've blown the bastard in half." He squeezed his eyes shut tight. His whole body wracked with the pain. Through gritted teeth he stifled a groan as best he could, then it seemed to ease off.

"Take care of Kate, Jack. There is no family left she can go to."

"You ain't under the dirt yet, Jim."

"Thanks, but both of us know I'm not going to be in church this Sunday."

I started to deny it, but sometimes you got to eat what's on the plate no matter how bad it tastes.

"She will always have a place here, Jim."

"Thanks my friend." He grasped my hand and shook it. I felt honored to have a friend of this caliber. This was a man.

Jim dozed off mercifully. You could hear the rattle in his breathing. After a while, Kathleen came back, and held his hand. Not knowing what to say, I patted her on the shoulder and went outside.

Rooster and I hogtied Vass Hart to a pack mule for the trip to the Lincoln county jail. We left when it was light enough to see the trail and headed north. Vass had taken most of a gun barrel load of the rock salt to the side of his face. He would have awful scarring, and it must have hurt like hell. His eye looked unfocused too. In spite of this, I felt no remorse.

We made good time, our only stops were to rest the horses and get a bite to eat. We lifted our guest off the pack horse, sat him on a rock, and untied his hands to eat. He stared at me remembering a court martial and the officer who conducted it.

"I remember you, Shane. You should have hung me."

"A mistake I'm going to fix," I said.

"Lincoln county jail?"

"Yep."

"How's my face?"

"Pretty bad. You got even uglier than you were."

"Can't see too good either."

"You brought this grief on yourself, Hart."

"Someday I'm going to bring grief home to you, Shane."

"Not likely, where you are going, but I got a rope waiting for you at Three Arrows anytime you want to try it on." There was something else I wanted to ask.

"Tell me something, Vass. Why didn't you speak in your own defense at your court martial?" There was a tremor of emotion on his face, and then it went blank. I saw the same fear in his eyes I had seen then. What secret could frighten him, a hardened outlaw more than a death sentence? Our conversation was over. Hard looks and curses accompanied us the rest of the trip.

We rode in to Lincoln early that evening, and turned our prisoner over to the sheriff to await trial. I wrote out a deposition and Rooster witnessed it. I promised to testify at the trial. Vass Hart was no stranger to the sheriff or the Lincoln county jail.

We decided to spend the night in Lincoln and return home tomorrow. I had some business to attend to, but it could wait until the next morning. We dropped our horses off at the livery stable, and went searching for a restaurant.

After supper, we split a bottle of awful saloon whiskey at the local watering hole. I offered to foot the bill for Rooster a sporting house visit, which he declined in favor of some shuteye. Neither of us was used to a bed, so we just bunked with the horses at the livery.

The next morning we carried two sore heads with us back to the same restaurant for a breakfast of biscuits, eggs, and side meat. There was even some gravy for the biscuits. I felt a hand on my shoulder and mine slipped under the table to my gun.

"Hello again, Captain Jack. Can I sell you some lingerie for the ladies at the ranch?" It was the little fat man who had stopped by the ranch. He had left before the fun began.

"Good to see you, Maxie. How's business?" I asked.

"Very, very good believe it or not. Not much competition in this territory, and you know the ladies are going to have their garments and unmentionables."

Rooster cocked an eye at me and started to speak, but I beat him to it. "Don't ask," I said.

Maxie joined us for breakfast, and actually seemed disappointed he had missed the events at Three Arrows, when Rooster told him of all that had transpired. His head bobbed when he laughed at our mock hanging, and soon Maxie was doing it too. Maxie told us if he were a dime novel author he could make a fortune with this story. He turned out to be a pretty good fellow. He promised to visit the ranch the next time he worked this territory, and would bring samples of his wares. Rooster told him he didn't care much for lingerie samples, but got a promise to bring some newspapers too.

Chapter 11

The assayer's jaw dropped to his belt buckle when I took the gold out of my saddlebags.

"Mister," he paused, "there ain't enough cash in this office to pay you what these nuggets are worth." He walked around the counter and threw the bolt on the door.

"No problem, I don't need a large amount of cash. A letter of credit to the bank will do nicely. Of course you can take your fees out of that account too," I said.

Beaming, he commenced placing nuggets on his scales, and writing a figure for each one. After an hour of; weighing, reweighing, and cyphering, he shook his head and said, "Captain Jack, you are one rich man."

It was a leading question, he was curious. I answered simply, "Yes, I am." Taking the letter of credit, I tipped my hat to him and left.

I walked across the street to the bank, and saw a group of riders coming down the middle of the street. Rafe Hall and Cliff Britt had their hands bound, and were escorted by the Lincoln county sheriff and a posse. They looked my way. I shook my head and kept walking.

Two men were standing by the bank doors, waiting for it to open. Both were dressed in suits and derby hats. They sported silver tipped canes and gold watch chains. Two pairs of squinted eyes stared at me, and the short one with no chin stared at me and snickered, while the tall skinny one was bent over slapping his knee and grinning like a jackass eating cactus.

"Good morning," they said in unison. The tall one was going to stretch his mouth if he held that grin much longer.

"I can see you are an enterprising man such as Mister Michael here and myself," said the tall one.

"What makes you say that?" I said.

"Simply, because you are ready to transact business the minute the bank door opens and they are causing an unwanted delay to you. Seize the day! The early bird gets the worm and all that eh? Allow us to introduce ourselves, my name is Wayne, and this is my partner, Mister Michael. We are co-owners of the M&W land company." Both men held their hands out. The bank teller opened the door and I walked by them ignoring their hands. I had met my first carpetbaggers.

I was escorted by the bank manager to his office, where I deposited my letter of credit, and promised to notify him in advance of any large withdrawal I might need. I left with assurances of security and discretion in all our transactions.

I met Rooster at the livery, and gave him the bonus money he would have been paid in Midland. He didn't want to take it, but I folded it and put it in his shirt pocket, and told him to enjoy it. We made plans to meet for supper, and I saw his eyes glance at the saloon down the street. He would be easy to find later.

Seeing those two vultures outside the bank door had gotten me concerned about where their greedy hands may have been. I walked down to the land office, and had the clerk open his ledger to my land sections.

"Mr. Shane, I see you've got some taxes that must be paid by the end of the year, or your ranch may be confiscated to pay them. Money is scarce since the war for most folks, and if the same is true of yourself, the M & W Land company would be more than glad to make you the same fair offer for your ranch as they have others. I'm sure of it," he said.

He smiled at me and I smiled back. Then I reached over his desk and pulled him out of his chair. I lifted him in the air as high as I could, and asked him in a soft voice, "Do you want to tell me how much those two M & W bastards pay you to point poor folks to them, or would you rather I throw your sorry ass through that glass window? You got to three. One…"

He started talking as fast as a chicken coop full of hens could cackle. His name was Feeney, and he got a nice kickback on every piece of land sold to M & W for a pittance of its worth, when the owners couldn't pay the taxes. Normally, I don't have a mean streak in me. If you rile me, you'll wish you hadn't, but I ain't mean. But there are situations sometimes which make me want to square the books. This was one of them.

I looked over the county maps until I found the most rugged piece of rocky desert land on record. No water, in fact, no nothing for fifty miles in any direction. Perfect.

"Feeney, I want to file a claim right here," I told him.

I went to the saloon to pick up Rooster. I had a couple of drinks while watching him entertain his audience of cowboys and farmers. The man had a gift for sure. He was telling a wild tail about a band of Indians that had chased him into a box canyon, and all he had to fight with was his straight razor. This had them all on the edge of their chairs, anxiously awaiting his next words. He continued his tale, his hand gestures leading their eyes and imaginations. He told how their captives would be scalped alive then tortured to horrible deaths. He stopped to roll a cigarette, much to the dismay of his listeners.

"Well what happened?" said a cowboy who couldn't stand the suspense any longer.

"I threw off my hat and shaved my head before they could get to me. When they saw me with that bald head; well they just got disgusted and left. It would be plumb shameful to have a scalp that looked like a piece of side meat hanging up outside your teepee." The serious look on his face turned into a grin, and he started laughing. The rest of the bar knew they had been had and joined him. Heads were going up and down everywhere.

At sundown, Rooster and I sat in the hotel dining room, dressed in our new western suits. Our new hats were on the rack by the door. We had the best rooms in the hotel. We sat by the window with our cigars and champagne, and the knowledge of what was to come made them taste sweeter. This was a day I planned to remember and enjoy for a lot of years.

Rooster said, "Do these two varmints look like a rat and a coyote?"

"You must see them walking down the street," I said. They were headed for the hotel as I expected. Fear of my wrath had induced Feeney to play his part as instructed.

Wayne and Michael came through the double doors of the hotel lobby, saw us, and made a beeline for our table. One was grinning and the other snickering. I'm glad I had already eaten my supper.

"This has to be a sign it was ordained we should meet," said the taller one, Wayne. The little one, Michael snickered as if this was very funny. Rooster was right, he did look like a rat.

"Why don't you gentlemen join us for some champagne and cigars?" I said, and didn't have to ask them twice. I offered them both a cigar, which they examined and exchanged looks. I had paid fifty-cents apiece for them and they knew it. If there had been more expensive ones available I would have bought them.

The conversation was of a general nature, with occasional questions directed at me about mining, or land acquisition. I let them casually interrogate me for the best part of an hour, before I decided to give them what they came for.

"Are you boys ready to get down to business, or do you want to keep pussyfooting around the stage? You've been dogging me all day trying to get your hands in my business, so if you have a business proposal I suggest you either put it on the table or call it a night," I said.

"Hmmmmmm, I was right about you. Knew it when I saw you. Simply put, Mr. Shane, there are no secrets in a small town." Wayne was doing all the talking; he must be the brains of the two. "It has come to our attention, through business circles of course, that you have some profitable interests in the mining sector. One could do himself a great service by inviting partners, with connections in the financial world, to invest and spread the risks involved in these ventures."

Like hell, I thought. This was a fox trying to talk his way into the hen house.

"Are you boys serious? I doubt you've got the capital to play on this level." I reached in my pocket and pitched a gold nugget across the table.

"We ain't talking dirt farmer ranches here. Put your cards on the table boys, or fold 'em. It's getting past my bedtime."

Wayne picked the nugget up and fondled it like a young girl's hand. He was hooked.

"Mister Michael and myself are in the game, sir. Call your shot."

I made a show out of resting my hands on my clasped fingers, as if coming to a decision.

"You boys better be on the square. I have a very rich claim, as I am sure you have seen the results of. It is surrounded by several square miles which probably have the same gold veins running through it. I intend to buy as much of this land surrounding my claim as I can. I don't mind using all my capital, but why think small? Every acre of land you buy for fifty dollars might yield fifty million."

"F-f-f-fifty m-m-million? Dollars?" Michael broke his silence sounding like an excited Lonnie Butterfield.

"Some may only yield a few thousand. Still, a substantial return on the dollar wouldn't you say?" I said.

Mister Wayne got to his feet and said, "I believe we have a deal my good man. Mister Michael and I must liquefy our holdings as quickly as possible. Would Friday be a good day to start our transactions?"

I assured them Friday would be perfect. They couldn't leave fast enough, with larceny in their hearts and too much greed in their minds, for them to work properly.

Rooster looked at me and said, "What just happened here? Those boys looked like you just gave them the key to the bank vault."

I laughed out loud, and said, "Those two crooks are going to find out exactly where my claim is tomorrow, when they question the land clerk, Feeney, who is more afraid of me than them. I told him to show them the location on the map. They are going to use every cent they can beg, borrow, or have stolen, to buy every acre around that claim of mine, with no thoughts of a partnership with me. They have no intention of meeting me on Friday, or sharing any profit with me. They only said that to give them time to sell every piece of land they have stolen from its rightful owners."

"Is there really a gold mine on that land?" asked Rooster.

"Not a chance. The land is worthless for anything but a rattlesnake farm. I picked it out for a claim, because it was the cheapest most rugged land on the map. They will pay fifty dollars an acre for land that sold for fifty cents an acre."

"I reckon someone is going to make a pretty fair profit. Wonder who owns it?"

I smiled at Rooster and said, "I do."

I had purchased the land under the ranch's name, instead of my own, with Feeney's and the bank's help. When the proceeds came in from the sale to those two carpetbaggers, I would get my money back. There would be enough profit to pay the taxes

on every farm and ranch on Feeney's books. There would also be two new prospectors in the desert wearing derby hats.

Life can be very good sometimes.

* * *

Two days later, Rooster and I were driving our new wagon full of supplies home to Three Arrows. When the ranch came in sight and the distance closed, I felt something wasn't right. As we approached the river, the reason for my unease was obvious. There was a horse standing under the cottonwoods at our small cemetery, and a fresh grave testified to Jim Sullivan's death bed prophecy. He had been right. He wouldn't be in church on Sunday.

Kathleen Sullivan was sitting on the ground next to Jim's grave. Sometimes there just aren't any words to say, so I didn't try. She arose and walked to meet us when we stopped the wagon and stepped down. Her eyes were red and swollen, and the tracks of recent tears lined each cheek. It hurt me to see her tormented so. Rooster and I shared her grief for Jim. He had been a good man. We gave hugs and walked over to the grave to pay our respects. After a silent moment, Rooster left with the wagon, and I stayed with Kathleen.

She said, "He never awakened yesterday morning. We said our goodbyes the night before at his insistence. Now I'm glad we did. It would have been worse if we hadn't. I didn't think you would mind him being buried here."

"I wouldn't have it any other way," I said and meant it, "How long have you been sitting here?"

"All day."

"Are you ready to walk back now?"

"I suppose I ought to. It will be dark soon. I need to make

some plans when I can think straight again. I hope you don't mind if I stay on a few days."

Deep down inside me I felt a knot pulled tight, and I wasn't sure why.

"Kate, the day Jim came off that porch, and put himself between Vass Hart's knife and Charley, was the day part of Three Arrows became yours. This is your home for as long as you want to be here."

She looked at me and said, "You mean that don't you."

"Yes, I do."

"When my head clears of grief I will think on it. I do not want to be a burden to you, Captain."

I had to chew my words a little before I let them out. What I was thinking was wrong. A good woman's husband was buried right here, and his body barely cold. All I trusted myself to mumble was, "No burden."

Chapter 12

"There's no way you can hit him from this distance, Cort," I said to the young man next to me lying spread-eagled with his Sharps rifle nestled into his shoulder. The rifle thundered and bucked, but his quarry was still standing. I watched from our position hundreds of yards away. I was about to say something when he read my mind and held his hand up.

"Wait," was all he said.

The antelope slowly knelt, and rolled on his side. Cort looked through the sight again and reloaded the Sharps. Another report echoed across the valley and produced the same result. I wondered how many times that rifle had sent men under during the war.

Lonnie, watching from behind said, "D-d-d-damn, Cort!"

I slapped him on the back, and said, "Damn good shooting, Cort."

He smiled at the compliment and said, "Tell Charley."

I was sure Cort was going to become a permanent part of our family before long, and that was fine by me. He pulled his weight and more. He usually took the lead and the other hands followed. He was young in years only. Charley and Cort had become a couple you had only to glance at, to know they were head over heels. Cort could shave a hair off a gnat's butt at five hundred yards with his Sharps, and Charley couldn't shoot a hole in the ceiling with a six shooter and a box of shells. I guess opposites do attract.

Cort and the Butterfield brothers rode down the valley, to the meadow where the two antelopes were lying. They would field dress them, and deliver the meat to Consuelo. She would work her magic in the cook house, and we would have antelope steaks on the table tonight.

I rode to the top of the cliffs, enjoying the view of the valley below. In the distance, I saw the new bunkhouse occupied by twenty plus hands now. The way the herd was growing we would need more riders this year. The cattle had fattened on the green valley meadows and were ready to be driven to market. Last year, Charles Goodnight and Oliver Loving established a cattle trail from Texas up the Pecos river valley to Fort Sumner, then on to Denver. John Chisholm had joined his cattle to them in the drive that would put their names in history books one day.

We added rooms to the ranch house for Rooster and me. He was doing the job of ramrod against his objections, but there was no one I would trust more to work the hands fairly. Juan's household had now doubled in size with two of Consuelo's sisters, and a brother in law moving in. Consuelo had become overworked when the cooking requirements more than tripled. She was delighted when I asked her if she could send for help. Her family members wouldn't hesitate to leave the border area, where poverty and violence lived on both sides of the river. Wounds from the war with Mexico hadn't healed before the North and South conflict brought new ones. As with all wars, the peons bore the brunt of the civilian suffering.

Her little garden had grown to the size of a small farm. Looking at the long straight rows, I could see the golden tassels on the corn waving in the breeze. Little Juan was loading vegetables into a cart as he picked them under his *tia's* watchful eye.

Her name was, Maria and Rooster had his watchful eye on

her, whenever he could. Any time I caught him bird dogging her I asked him if he was working on his Spanish.

I would be rewarded with that wondrous laugh, and a response of, *"Si."*

Down by the river, I saw a female rider walking her mare by the cottonwoods. The sorrel coat on the mare was almost as red as the rider's long hair. She dismounted at the little plot of graves, and tied her horse to the fencing we had built around it. Green grass grew thick over Jim Sullivan's grave. The fresh picked yellow sunflowers Kate placed on the grave accented the color.

We talked often. She could converse intelligently on almost everything, and I found myself asking her advice on a multitude of subjects from Charley to ranch operations. Sometimes, we just sat together under the cottonwoods visiting the graves. There are a lot of ways to talk. A personal line existed between us that had never been crossed. Some wounds were still too tender to touch. She never had given me her answer about staying. I guess she was still studying on it. I turned my buckskin down the trail to the bottom of the cliffs and rode toward the cemetery.

A dead man and woman kept our lives on a short rope. It had to be cut if we were ever to move on and live them. Dark memories existed in the valley between us, daring us to venture closer to each other. I dismounted and tied my horse to the fence rail. She raised her head and faced my direction.

"Kate," I greeted her and took off my hat.

"Captain," she replied.

"Nice day, ain't it?"

"Early summer or is it late spring?"

"I'll go with summer, not much romance in the air."

"What are you suggesting, Captain Shane?"

"Nothing, just that the birds and animals have finished pairing up for this year."

"Oh, I, uh, thought," she colored slightly, and turned toward the graves.

"Kate, I never was a smooth talker when it came to gals so forgive me if I said something wrong."

"No, no, it's just me. I think maybe it's time for me to leave Three Arrows."

At the battle of Atlanta in 1864, I had a horse shot out from under me while galloping across a bridge at night. I was thrown from the saddle over the wooden rails of the bridge siding. As I flew through the dark, I was disoriented, not knowing what was below in the dark to meet my fall, until I plunged into deep water. When I came to the surface, I knew it wasn't my day to die, and the water had saved me. This time there wasn't any water. I was drowning.

Words wouldn't come out of my mouth when I needed them the most. I stood there silently while she mounted her mare, and rode away towards the house. I sat down on the ground. I was having feelings I didn't understand going through my head.

The next morning, Kate had Rooster drive her and her wagon to Lincoln, where she would hire a driver to continue her journey to California. She never said goodbye or looked back. I'd been a damned fool for thinking what I had been thinking.

Chapter 13

I loaded a pack mule with supplies, saddled my buckskin, and strapped on my guns. I planned to lose myself in the back country for a while. I had a lot of things in my head that needed to get out of it. I was kind of hoping I'd run into some more Indians or bandits. I wasn't looking for fun this time.

The next few days I wandered south down into Texas. Drinking sour mash coffee in the mornings failed to dissolve the dreams I awoke from. The whiskey didn't drown them out at night either. Drifting south, I rode into Fort Stockton late one afternoon. The streets were full of freighters, and merchants lined the boardwalk outside their shops. Stock workers sat on the corral fences, and buffalo soldiers from the 9th Cavalry were all over town. I rode down to the springs named after the Comanche trail they were located on, and watered my horse. For a dollar, the livery stable boarded my horse and mule. I gave the man an extra two-bits to give them some extra oats. I hadn't been very good company for them the last few days.

There was a small saloon among the shops and I entered it. Greeting me were the smells of beer and whiskey and sawdust. And something else, perfume.

It was a sunny day outside and I was blind when I entered the darkened interior. A voice in the shadow spoke to me, "I like big handsome cowboys, but not in my lap. Sit down here at the table before you stumble over me and bounce us both off the floor. With my reputation, no one would ever believe I was down there by accident,"

"Thanks," I said, feeling the back of a chair and sitting down. As my eyes adjusted, I stared into the eyes of a young woman with coal black hair grown down to her waist. She looked as good as her perfume smelled.

"Where are you from, handsome?"

"Up north, Lincoln way." I said.

"Willie, bring us a couple of beers."

"Add a couple of glasses and a bottle too, Willie."

In a minute, Willie brought a tray with two beer mugs foaming, a bottle of whiskey and two glasses.

"A toast to you, ma'am." I lifted the mug to my lips and drained it.

"Thirsty cowboy?"

"Just washing the dust off inside."

Her leg found mine under the table. Her eyes turned soft and she whispered in my ear.

"Got anything else needs dusting off, cowboy? My name is, Stormy."

* * *

It's always nice to start the day with a roll in the hay. It was livery stable hay and I was by myself, but it was going to be a good day. Sore knuckles and all.

Last night was a little fuzzy in places on account of the several beers and shots of whiskey I drank. Stormy was easy to talk to, and she wasn't the "soiled dove" she acted toward customers. I had invited her to eat supper with me and she accepted. She took my arm and we strolled down the street to the restaurant she recommended. The meal was good and we got lots of looks from the other patrons. I was a stranger and Stormy was known by reputation. People tend to gossip and a reputation is easy to get in a small town like Fort Stockton, whether deserved or not.

We walked back to the saloon and trouble. Two cowboys were waiting at the makeshift bar made of planks and barrels. They had come in and started drinking whiskey before we left for supper. From the looks of them, they hadn't slowed down in our absence.

"Evenin' ma'am," said the taller one.

"Good evening boys," answered Stormy, "is the bartender taking care of you?"

"Yeah, but we was thinking you might do a better job of it."

"Then grab a table and let me know what you're drinking."

"It ain't a table we're needing, it's a poke we're wanting."

"Fellow, I'd like to forget you said that. Don't get any wrong ideas about me because we are in a saloon."

He sauntered over to us. He was an arrogant drunk who should have apologized for his behavior, and went back to his drinking. I could see it wasn't going to happen. Some men are thick-headed and some stubborn. This one was crossbred a heavy dose of both.

"C'mon darlin', let's you and me and Little Elmer go out back to your crib or wherever, and have us a party. We got money in our pockets for you, and that ain't all!"

My fist was the last thing he saw. I swung from the floor and nailed him solid on the chin. The ground shook when he hit it. I heard a gun hammer click and looked up to see Little Elmer nervously pointing a pistol at me.

"Ya killed Cletis." His hand was shaking and he was drunk. I had to stop this before it got started.

"Little Elmer! Does Big Elmer know you and your brother are at a saloon in town drinking? Does your mother know how you talk to women?"

I saw the wheels turning behind wide eyes. I had him off balance now.

"Put that gun in your holster right now, and help me get your brother out of here."

He hesitated; obviously he was used to big brother making the decisions for both of them. I had enough of this. I moved my hand to my gun.

"Do it! Holster that gun or you'll be dead before you hit the floor."

Somewhere in his head a light came on. The gun barrel lowered. He took the hammer off cock and holstered the gun. We laid his brother across his horse and Little Elmer mounted his. I pointed both of them toward home with a story to tell. I'd like to hear their version when it was told to Big Elmer.

I went back inside, and Stormy led me to a table in the back. Whiskey and glasses appeared. She poured me a drink, and laid her hand on mine.

"It's been a long time since this gal got treated like a lady, Jack. You've treated me respectable by taking me out in public today, buying me supper, and even fighting for my honor. You better not hang around here too long, or I ain't gonna be able to let you go."

"I didn't mean to cause any trouble, but he shouldn't have said those things to you."

"Jack, lots of men come in here and get the idea I'm easy because I'm inside these walls. There's a sporting house down the street, and those gals don't look any different than I do. The difference is I'm not a whore, and I own this saloon. The bartender works for me. It's hard for a woman to make a living by herself. I had enough money to build this place, such as it is, and buy enough stock to get started."

I spent the next few hours sipping the good whiskey she kept under the counter, and telling her about my ranch, the people there, and Kathleen. She told me about coming west from New Orleans after the war. Like so many others, the war had taken her father and their property. This was just a stop on the way to the rest of her life, she said.

Closing time came. She sent the bartender home and started locking up for the night. She looked at me and didn't speak for a moment as if collecting her thoughts.

"Cowboy, if I thought you would stick around I'd rope you and lead you home. Whether you know it or not, you want your Three Arrows brand on another woman. Kathleen Sullivan is a very lucky woman, and I don't know why she ever left a man like you. Now don't say a word, just give me one kiss before you walk out the door. I want to remember this night for a long time."

Chapter 14

The man with the badge pinned on his shirt said, "I'm looking for a man name of Jack Shane," he looked me over good and said, "would that be you by any chance, cowboy?"

He didn't know me from Adam. I could finish saddling my horse and ride off. If he thought I was wanted for something, his hand would be resting on his gun and he wouldn't be alone. It wasn't like that. I was curious who might be looking for me.

"It just might be. What can I do for you, deputy?" I answered.

"The sheriff sent me around to see if there were any strangers in the livery, they usually all pass through here. They've got a wire for you at the telegraph office. It must be important because he said it had been sent out all over the area trying to find you."

No one including myself had known where I was going. If someone went to this much trouble to locate me it wasn't good news. I followed the deputy to the telegraph office, and found out how right I was.

The telegram read: UNKA JACK COME QUICK STOP KATHLEEN AND ROOSTER MISSING STOP CHARLEY.

It was dated four days ago. I could make it back in three with a couple of extra horses to swap out. I headed back to the livery stable.

The two horses I bought from the livery owner were good

mounts and worth their price. I started immediately and made a lot of miles before dark. I swapped horses twice to keep them rested.

Traveling gives a man plenty of time to study on things. In a big desolate country like this, people can easily disappear without a trace. There are a lot of places to be hidden, but not many reasons to, except for the human ones. A lone rider might be thrown or lose a horse, but not two people in a wagon. That left outlaws, Indians, and Mexican bandits.

Since Vass Hart was in prison waiting on his trip up the gallows stairs, there hadn't been any reports of outlaws. The Comanche raiding parties since the war had stopped when most of the tribes had been moved on reservations in the Indian Nations. I hoped for Kathleen's and Rooster's sake it was something else. Mexican bandits roamed the nearby hills southwest to the border towns on the Rio Grande. There was a good chance they were captured and being held for ransom. If they were Comancheros trading with the Indians, a red headed woman like Kate was worth a lot of horses, no matter who had her. They wouldn't have any reason to keep Rooster alive though. Not much of a market for old cowboys. If such is the case; I will do whatever it takes to get them back.

I reckoned bandits or Comancheros would make for the border somewhere southeast toward Juarez. There were several small towns and villages on the other side of the river. I might cut their trail in a couple of days if I pushed the horses, and had a whole lot of luck. The wire was four days old when I received it. Add at least a day to know for sure they were missing, and this day I had spent traveling. Six days. They would have discarded Kathleen's wagon, because it was too easy to follow and would slow them down. There would be a small camp somewhere on their journey back, where they kept prisoners and stolen contraband until this raid was finished. If I could find that camp, Kathleen and Rooster had a chance. And I had an idea how to find it.

As soon as it was light enough, I started at a good pace and held it most of the day. I stopped to rest the horses at noon, in the shade of a mesa. I was going to ask a lot of them today, but I wasn't going to kill them if I didn't have to.

It was getting twilight when I reached the high mesa I had been riding toward since I spotted it on the horizon. By the time I got the horses unsaddled and tethered, it was almost dark. I took my saddle off the one I was riding, and fed and watered them all.

I began the long climb up the mesa. It wasn't that rigorous, a long walk up the gentleslope side. An hour later, I reached the top in the dark and sat down on a rock. Two days of hard riding from Fort Stockton had covered a lot of miles. Tomorrow should have me close if I guessed right.

The wind picked up. As always, the temperature started dropping as soon as the sun went over the horizon. It would be cold in the morning. Chilly enough for a big fire. One you could see for miles if you were high enough.

The desert sky at night is a wonder I never grew tired of watching. Millions of stars each homesteading their little pieces of heaven as far as you could see. The desert itself hinted at mystery. Strange lights moved across the desert floor, and the music of the winds orchestrated their symphonies through the rocks and canyons.

What if I were wrong about the bandits? Maybe there were Indians involved, or maybe Rooster had enough of ranching, and decided to drive Kate's wagon to California for her.

My mind was going in circles. It pained me to think about any harm coming to Kathleen. Images of her and a woman with long black hair kept chasing each other in my thoughts. Did Kate want to disappear somewhere I would never find her?

I slept fitfully, wrapped in a blanket to protect from the cold night wind up this high. I sat against a tall rock in the sand which knocked some of the wind off of me. Several times during the night, I searched in all directions for the light of a campfire. When I found none, I would grab another nap. I was waiting for enough light to climb down when I saw it. It wasn't much, and it was a lot of miles away, but it was a fire. I took a compass reading and hoped it was the campfire I was looking for.

Chapter 15

Rooster

If I'd had the scattergun, it'd be Armando on the ground instead of me. This old cowboy could have taken him out of the saddle with one good arm. The blood crusted on my sleeve looks bad, but I think the bullet wound has quit bleeding. It does smart a mite.

Don't know why they didn't send me under back there where they jumped us. I expect it had something to do with Miss Kate's fast thinking. She yelled at them to leave her husband alone. I felt proud they thought I was him, even if I was shot.

Bullets or worse are waiting for me after they trade her off. Armando, the leader and the one they call Goyo, like to wave their machetes at you. I don't like the looks they are giving me.

These ropes are sure tight. Somebody in Mexico learned a whole lot about knot tying. It kind of reminds me of my time aboard ship in the old days. When I was a young pistol ball, old Salty taught me rigging and knot tying. One of those things he taught me was a good knot is easy to untie too.

If these hellions do like they did yesterday morning, as soon as coffee and beans are done they'll be off to raise more hellfire and thievery. That will be the time to try to escape, and get Miss Kate away from them. There are plenty of horses to choose from for our getaway, if I can take care of Goliath up there on the rock. Damned if that ain't the biggest Mexican I ever seen.

So long as they don't catch on that my Spanish is tolerable, they might say something in front of me that will help us. Glad I learned to speak a little Mex back when I was chasing cows on the border, and those days sailing up and down the coast from Florida, all the way down to the Cape.

I'd probably still be sailing if we hadn't run aground near Galveston. Lucky for me I made it to shore. I almost drowned. I got even luckier when some good old boys found me, and put a rope in one hand and reins in the other. I could use some of that luck right now.

Funny how things fall in place for you sometimes, whether you're trying to make the pieces of a man's life fit or not. All the miles I had behind me, standing on a deck or sitting on a saddle, and I never seen anyplace I wanted to light for more than a few days. Then I saw Three Arrows. The valley, the people, and now Maria. All the pieces fit, and chances are I'll never get to see them again.

Chapter 16

The campfire I saw from the top of the mesa was several miles away. I rode toward it with compass in hand and long gun handy. My instincts told me it was the right one, but it could easily be some drifters or an old prospector trying his luck. I had to play my cards the way I saw them, and do it quick if I were to have any chance of finding my friends. A little bit of luck wouldn't hurt either.

It was dawn. The morning breeze picked up and fortune favored me as it blew from the direction I headed. I trusted my compass to point me in the general direction, and the smell of campfire smoke to warn me when I got close.

The area was rocky, and scattered with cactus, mesquite, and creosote which made traveling in a straight line impossible. It was slow going. The Three Arrows hands would be out searching, and it was possible I would cut their trail before I got to the campfire.

At noon I caught my first whiff of smoke. Not much, but it was there. I looked upwind but couldn't see anything yet. I tied the horses to some mesquite trees, and decided to go the rest of the way on foot or on my belly.

The desert sun had me soaked with sweat, and you could feel the heat coming off the rocks. It was stifling. I gave the horses some water and took a long drink myself. It was time to get started. Crouching and crawling, it was slow going approaching the camp. I couldn't rise up for risk of being seen. I followed the odor of smoke upwind until I saw it in the distance, then continued to sneak closer.

By the time I had gotten close, I was caked with dirt and sand. My boots looked like porcupines with the cactus needles sticking in them. I was going to feel like a fool if all I found was a couple of cowboys.

Five minutes later, I knew it wasn't cowboys, and I was going to kill somebody. Rooster's and Kathleen's heads were lying on the sand. A red rage overwhelmed me. It was killing time. I took my guns out and checked the loads. I wanted all of them.

Why hadn't I spoke to Kathleen when I could have? I should have told her how I felt about her, and talked her into staying at Three Arrows like I'd promised Jim. It was too late for talk now. It was time to play *El Deguello*, the song Santa Anna had played the morning of the massacre at the Alamo. It was killing time...with no quarter.

A grunt like a *javelina* rooting got my attention. Kathleen's head opened its eyes and that damn near put me over the edge. The other head made the *javelina* sound again, then snorted and opened up his eyes. My friends were buried in the sand up to their necks to keep them from escaping. With tears in my eyes, I had to stifle my laughter to stay hidden. They were alive!

Until Rooster snorted like a wild pig, I was ready to wipe out the whole bunch. I had a second chance to set things straight now and I was going to. First I had to get a couple of people unburied.

I took a long slow look at the camp; there was a small branch corral holding a dozen horses built against a rock wall, two wagons probably full of contraband next to the fence, a small woodpile next to a smoldering campfire with a cook pot over it, a crude lean-to with several bedrolls rolled up in its shade, and a huge Mexican standing on the top of a rock with a rifle. The guard.

The bedrolls meant there were several more bandits to be accounted for. The single saddle on the corral fence told me this was the only guard. This was going to be easy I thought.

I was out of pistol range and needed to get a lot closer to do any shooting. If the guard knew I was hiding this close in the brush, there would be hell to pay from his long gun. There was too much open space between us for me to rush him, therefore, I needed to work myself around behind him in the rocks. I started to crawl in that direction when the sound of horses galloping made me bury myself deeper in the brush.

"Diego!" The lead rider called. The bandits rode in trailed by a ball of dust painting everything in its path. Wearing a sombrero large enough for Kathleen to use as a parasol, the giant guard who stood on the rock waved to his *amigo*.

"Armando!"

The leader looked at Rooster and Kathleen, obviously enjoying their discomfort. He dismounted, and I heard the jingle of his boot spurs approaching them.

"You are comfortable, *Si?*" he said.

"You wouldn't want to loan me that sombrero would you, *amigo?*" Rooster replied.

"Forgive me *senor*, I have only the one and it is busy on my head."

"If you'll pardon me, I think I'll get back to my *siesta* now."

"If I wanted to, *gringo*, I could give you a long *siesta* with my machete. You are already buried." Armando turned to the others laughing at his joke.

Rooster lowered his head and closed his eyes. Armando

shifted his position between the sun and Kathleen, his shadow protecting her face. He bent down and held up a lock of red hair. In a quick movement, he parted the lock with his machete, and held it in front of her face.

"*Senora*', my heart will break if I see this hanging on the front of a teepee. Is there no one to pay a ransom for you?"

Kate stared ahead. I was sure her teeth were imbedded in that Irish tongue of hers. After a moment, Armando opened his fingers and let the wind take the hair from his hand as if it was her fate.

Chapter 17

In a shootout, a dozen guns against three are bad odds, especially when two of the three are buried up to their necks. There would be a better chance of escape after dark or tomorrow morning.

I wanted to let Rooster and Kathleen know of my presence. I found a flat rock, and with my knife, etched the Three Arrows Brand, >>> on it. I crawled underneath the mesquite bushes until I was in their line of sight. Working my way close to them, I leaned the rock against the base of a bush, where it could only be seen, at ground level.

I made my way back to the horses, and waited for dusk. It would be easier returning after dark when I could walk most of the way to their camp. I leaned against a rock in the shade and took a *siesta*.

I was up before dark, I fed the horses and saddled the buckskin. He would be ready to run when we returned. It was a lot easier walking back to the bandit's camp in the cool night air. I could see the campfire in the distance, and hear loud conversation and laughter. The wind brought smells from the cook fire that stirred my hunger. I crawled closer to the camp in the dark. There was another guard on the rock, and another on the wagon. A bottle of whiskey, probably tequila, was being passed around with supper. Apparently life was treating this bunch very well. Nothing for me to do but wait and watch. At least the coolness of the night air would bring relief to Kathleen and Rooster.

I watched as all but two of the bandits spread their bedrolls underneath the lean-to. The other two took up their rifles for night guard. One atop the big rock that Diego was on earlier, and the other on the wagon. Something important was in that wagon if they needed two guards. It was obvious their two prisoners couldn't escape on their own. Were they expecting me? No one knew I was coming, but maybe the men from Three Arrows had been seen searching for their two missing members. Or maybe they were guarding against more of their own kind.

There was no way I could take out both guards without the risk of awakening the others. Kathleen and Rooster would bare their wrath if I didn't succeed. I would wait until dawn, on the chance both guards would fall asleep, and I could dig my friends out.

I was having no luck tonight. A couple of hours before dawn the guards awakened Diego then climbed into their own bedrolls. Disappointed, I walked back to my small camp and did the same.

The sound of horses galloping made me throw off the blanket and grab my gun. I could see four horses traveling away from the camp. Going on another raid probably. Stealth wasn't doing me any good. It was time to meet this situation head on.

I mounted my horse and walked him to the bandit's camp. The sun was coming up behind me. I was almost there when Diego spotted me. I raised both hands in the air and kept going. His rifle held steady on me as I rode in.

"*Senor*, I think you are a lost and unlucky *hombre*." he said looking down from his rock perch.

"And I think you talk *macho* behind the gun." I stared him in the eyes, "Not enough *cajones* to meet me *mano e mano*, Diego?" I tied my horse to a mesquite bush and unbuckled my gun belt. I hung it on the saddle pommel and motioned with my hand for him to come to me. It was too much of an insult for one his size to ignore.

"I will show you who has the *cajones, amigo,*" he said. He laid his rifle down carefully and leaped off the rock to meet me.

Most big men are used to bowling over others, and using brute strength to win the contest. Because of this, they never have to develop their fighting skills. This was the case with Diego. I sidestepped his charge and let him have a fist in the gut as he went past. He turned and swung a fist at me that could crush rocks. I ducked and came up inside it with an uppercut right on the chin. It staggered him. His eyes showed he was beginning to understand he had bought into more than he bargained for.

"You are quick *amigo,* but they call me *El Toro* with good reason. You are not the *matador, Si?*" He came at me again expecting the same sidestep. Instead, I stepped to the other side and gave him an elbow to the temple as he passed. He fell to his knees, dazed. It was time to end this before he got lucky, and took my head off. I jumped in front of him, and gave him one on the chin with all I had. At first I thought he hadn't even felt it. Then his eyes rolled backwards and he fell face down with the impact of a large boulder. He was done.

"Well, I reckon you'll have to do until a real bull fighter comes along." I heard a voice behind me say. I turned around and saw Rooster looking at me chuckling. Kathleen had tears in her eyes. I buckled my gun belt on and went to find a shovel.

When I got back, Diego was sitting up rubbing his chin. I dropped the shovel next to him. With his digging and my pulling we got them both out of the ground. He motioned for them to come to the lean-to. He handed them both canteens. While they drank, he poured water in a large bowl and brought it to Kathleen with a towel. She nodded and took it to the privacy of some rocks. This act of compassion was not the act of a hard core *bandito.*

"Diego, you don't have the cut of a bandit, what are you doing with this bunch?" I asked.

"*Senor*, my family was very poor, and now they have left Mexico. Armando told me he had a place for me with his men. He said I was to be a guard. I swear on the cross I did not know he was a robber and kidnapper. If I try to leave now he will kill me."

"Have you ever worked cattle, or sheep, or done any farming?"

"*Si*, my family used to farm before they left."

"Help me get my friends home safe, and you can throw your bedroll in the bunkhouse on my ranch."

He made up his mind pretty quick. He had his horse saddled and his bedroll behind it five minutes later.

"What's in the wagon over there?" I said.

"Guns and bullets Armando stole from the army. He will sell them on the border where there is always a market for them."

"Maybe he won't this time."

We loaded Kathleen and Rooster on horses since they were in no shape to walk. I threw the remaining bedrolls in the wagon and a shovel full of hot coals from the campfire on top of them. It was time for us to get out of there.

We were almost to my camp when the wagon blew. Pieces of rifles were raining down behind us, and small explosions were going off. We turned our horses toward Three Arrows.

* * *

Kathleen

When I saw the rock under the bush with the Three Arrows brand etched in it, I knew only Jack could have placed it there. I

knew he would come. How could he have gotten so close
without being seen?

It's my fault Rooster is wounded and we were kidnapped. If
I hadn't been headstrong, and insisted on leaving Three Arrows,
we never would have met the bandits. But how could I ever
explain to Charley and the other women at the ranch I was in
love with Jack, and Jim just a year in the grave?

The irony of it, was I had asked Rooster to turn the wagon
around and take me home to the ranch. I never should have left.
I can see now Jack was having as hard a time as I was revealing
our feelings. I've always heard pride goeth before a fall, and I
fell in up to my neck. Literally.

It was daylight when Jack rode up to camp. Something
about him demands you respect him. When Diego charged him,
I never saw Jack move his fist. He put the big man down fast.
Some men would have shot him or sent him into the desert, but
not Jack. Like I said about demanding respect, Diego was soon
following him as I am sure the men under his command did
during the war.

I'm ashamed of the trouble I've caused, and don't know what
to say to him. I can't talk yet, but I will. And when I do I'll tell
him I'm in love with him.

* * *

At midmorning, we saw a dust cloud behind us approaching
with a vengeance. It was Armando and his fellow cutthroats in
pursuit. We were out manned and out gunned, and I had blown
up a wagon load of guns and ammunition they had stolen.

We can keep running and hope for luck or make a stand. If it
comes down to a shootout I stand a chance of losing Kate and
Rooster. All I can do is drop back alone, and hold them off while
they make a run for Three Arrows.

An hour later there was no doubt the bandits would catch

us. The distance between us was closing, and there would be hell to pay if they captured us. I looked at Rooster. He knew what I had to do and nodded. I reigned in my horse and dismounted, drawing my long gun as I did. I slapped the buckskin on the rear with my hat to keep him running with the other horses. I had no use for him now, but the others might. I lay on the ground using a large rock for cover and a stand to shoot from. I took the lead rider out of the saddle with my first shot. I jumped when I felt someone reach behind me and pull my Colt from its holster. It was Kathleen.

"You're not getting away this easy, Jack Shane" she said.

"Darling, it seems to me you were the one trying to get away."

"Look at me, Jack."

I turned my head and her lips were on mine. She pulled away and said, "Quit arguing and start shooting if you ever want another one of those."

She was right, they were almost on us. She started firing my pistol and I fired the Henry as fast as I could chamber rounds. We hit two more before I ran out of ammunition and heard the Navy Colt's hammer hitting on empty chambers. I pushed her behind me and took the Bowie knife out of my boot. We might go under, but I was going to make it cost to send us there. I picked up a large rock to throw at the first one's head when I charged him with the Bowie. Kathleen held the Colt by its barrel. She was ready to hammer someone's teeth in.

As they rode closer, I could see Armando's grinning jackass face. The grin disappeared when his sombrero flew off his head. The echo of a rifle reached us. We heard the gallop of several horses behind us now, and a hail of bullets peppered the dust made by the bandits' sudden retreat. Three Arrows was here!

Cort Benner and several other hands rode by us with their guns booming. The questions I wanted to ask the redhead in my arms would wait until later. Rooster returned with our horses, and it wasn't long before the sounds of gunshots diminished, and our rescuers rode back to us with grinning faces. The last they had seen of the bandits were the tails of their horses racing toward the border. Two of them were slumped over in the saddle and one without his sombrero.

It was a long ride back to Three Arrows. With every mile we came closer, another piece of my life fell into place. I told this to the smiling redhead riding next to me and she echoed my feelings. Cort and the boys had searched for Kathleen and Rooster since their disappearance. When they saw our dust in the distance they rode to investigate. They heard the gunshots and were met by a wounded Rooster who spurred them to our rescue.

Kate tended to Rooster's arm. She cleaned his wound and tied a makeshift bandage around it. My friend was pale and his eyes showed his pain. He rode in silence which told He he was suffering. I knew he was hurt bad with his normal sense of humor and banter absent. He needed a sawbones or he might lose that arm.

At a small stream we stopped to water the horses and rest. One of the hands made a pot of coffee over a small fire, and we ate some biscuits and jerky the former hostages wolfed down. The bandit bastards had fed them barely enough to keep them alive. I would have to pay Armando a visit one day.

Kathleen and I took a walk to have some conversation. Maybe the words would come out right this time. We rounded a small rise between us and the hands, which offered some privacy. I took her hand in mine.

"I didn't want you to leave," I said.

"I didn't want to," she said.

Two sentences and I was already lost.

"Was it something I said that made you leave?"

"Before we were ambushed by the bandits I had asked Rooster to turn the wagon around and return to Three Arrows."

Kate read the confusion on my face. "Jack, Jim's only been dead a year, and if I stayed near you...well there would be a time we might you know...get together. When that happened, Charley and the other women would hate me. I couldn't bear Charley looking at me like that. Do you understand?"

"Kate, it's different here than back east. Folks know it's a hard life being alone, and many a widow has married a week after her husband's funeral with nothing thought or said about it."

"Can you keep anything from happening between us, Jack?" she said.

"Nope."

"Then what?" I took her in my arms and kissed her. She didn't resist.

"I'm not like that."

"Like what?"

"You know...easy."

"You could be if you were married."

"M-m-married? Am I hearing you right, Jack?"

"Just say yes, Jack."

"Yes, Jack."

"When I first saw you buried in the sand at the bandit camp I thought you were dead, and something felt like it was dying in me. When you opened your eyes it came back to life I made a promise to myself not to lose you again. I love you, Kathleen."

"I love you, Jack."

"Let's go home, sweetheart."

Chapter 18

The homecoming at Three Arrows reminded me what a lucky man I was. Riders had ridden ahead to tell them the good news, and everyone was outside awaiting our arrival. The smoke from Consuelo's kitchen chimney carried the smells of dinner, and made my stomach growl. It had been awhile since I had eaten anything, and Kate and Rooster were in dire need of nourishment. Charley was jumping up and down with joy, and every face smiled at us.

Maria ran from the kitchen towards Rooster with arms open wide. I could see him trying to hide his wounded arm from her, but to his surprise she ran past him to Diego. The big Mexican lifted her up and gave her a big hug and a kiss on the cheek. She then turned to Rooster and discovered his wounded arm.

"*El Gallo* is trying to get himself killed to get away from his *gallina, si?*" she said.

"Looks to me like you just met someone else." Women baffled him as much as they do me.

"*El stupido!* That is *mi hermano!*" Diego was her brother. She kissed Rooster on his lips and his ears turned red. She grabbed Diego's hand to guide him to the kitchen to be reunited with his other sisters, and with the other hand she held Rooster tight by his good arm, and giving him what for in two languages.

I hugged Charley and passed her to Kathleen. In that secret language women use to communicate with, one look told

Charley there was going to be a permanent addition to our family. With arms linked and chatting happily, the two of them went inside the house, already making plans. I headed toward the kitchen with plans of my own.

The sawbones showed up the next morning to attend to Kate and Rooster. Kate's health had been taxed by her treatment from the bandits, but nothing a long warm bath and a few days of rest and good food wouldn't cure. Rooster was a different story. The gunshot wound to his arm was serious. He wasn't going to lose the arm, but he'd thrown his last rope over a cow. My friend would never complain. He would joke about it instead. There was a lot more to Rooster than met the eye.

He was lying on his bed resting. The sawbones had cleaned the wound and stitched it closed. There was a clean bandage over it and the arm was in a sling. Maria would make sure it was cleaned and dressed daily. He sat up when I came into the room we shared. I sat in a chair next to his bed trying to look strict and stern.

"I guess you think you can lie around all day anymore. And right after you had a holiday," I said.

"A man's got to have his rest and his fun."

"Don't get lazy on me. You don't get paid fifty dollars a month to break in a new bed."

"I don't get paid fifty dollars a month for anything. If you got any ideas of hiring me as a fast gun, I got some bad news for you. You can time my quick draw with a calendar now."

"What I got in mind for you doesn't include your lightning fast gun play."

"Cap'n Jack, you know I'll ride for the Three Arrows brand even if it is single handed." We both laughed out loud at his joke. I knew he would always be Rooster, even with a stiff wing.

"You are going to earn every penny of it, my friend. Every penny."

"I know you ain't offering me any charity cause you know

how I'd feel about that, but I'm getting plumb nervous thinking about how hard I might have to work for fifty dollars a month."

"I want to hire your eyes and ears along with your judgment. Three Arrows is growing faster than I can manage it by myself. I trust you to keep abreast of our activities, and make decisions with the ranch's best interests in mind."

"Hell, you get that for twenty dollars a month now."

"One more condition I hope you agree to."

"What is it?"

"Plan on living here as family from now on," I said.

The operation of a working ranch never stops for battles with nature, men, or death. Cows and cowboys have to be fed, calves branded, horses shod, fences repaired and a hundred other chores. Life goes on every day with simple repetition of the days before, and it pauses for only the most important of activities...like a wedding. The preacher had been summoned, and the date of his expected arrival set the wedding plans in motion. Friends from neighboring ranches and farms, and a few friends from town had been invited. To our surprise and pleasure, Maxie, the lingerie salesman, rode in when he heard of the celebration Three Arrows planned. As promised, he brought free samples of his wares for the ladies and newspapers for Rooster. He was soon surrounded by our womenfolk who explored his catalogs with their eyes wide and girlish giggles. He had a package for Kate. She saw my stare, and her green eyes flashed a message I read loud and clear. I would be seeing the contents of the package later. Was it getting warmer this evening or is it just me?

Chapter 19

Vass Hart

They sent the same boy to stand guard again tonight. He don't know he's the one being watched. If I had my pig sticker he would never see it coming. Just like the captain and his little princess are going to get a surprise when Rafe and Cliff and me get out of here. I almost had her that night of the raid. I would have too, except for that devil flying into me. The time will come when she has to answer for what she did to me.

My day of reckoning is coming. Mister Captain Jack Shane, you scarred me and blinded me, and made women cringe and children run for their mamas when they see me. You should have killed me twice now when you had the chance, because I ain't about to give you another one.

You asked me what I had to hide. You know I have a secret, but you damn sure don't know what it is and I ain't gonna let you find out. It's my secret, not yours. Worth more than gold to me.

Speaking of gold, how does a Johnny Reb war veteran buy a herd of over a thousand head when he has been in the war for years? The pay ain't that good even for an almighty captain.

Tales have been told about Confederate gold missing. Could that be it? Maybe you found some war chest buried. The colonel tells me we could resurrect the cause if we had the backing. Not that I give a damn about any cause except Vass Hart, but it could put a man in a position to indulge himself in whatever power and pleasures he enjoys. We might have to talk some business, Captain Jack.

"Hey boy, want to play some cards with us? Come on over to the cell bars."

Chapter 20

"Would you like a blindfold or for me to roll you a cigarette, Cap'n Jack?"

"Rooster, I've been in tighter situations than this. I'm not nervous, so quit your kidding."

"When you was in those tight situations, did you put your hat on backwards and wear boots that don't match? Was that to give you an edge?"

"I haven't finished getting dressed is all." I looked down at the mismatched boots. He had me. We both laughed. I swapped my work boot for the dress boot. We were dressed for the wedding in the suits we had purchased in Lincoln for the carpetbaggers' benefit.

The preacher had arrived this morning to perform the ceremony. He promised to keep us in his circuit for any future services we might require, and he also believed an occasional "hell-fire" sermon wouldn't do the ranch hands any harm either.

The ceremony was held on the house yard, with Rooster standing up for me. Charley of course, was Kate's lady in waiting, doing whatever ladies in waiting do. Another one of those things men don't understand. There was a large crowd of neighbors, friends, and Three Arrows hands assembled. We said our vows and the men gathered around us and smiled, while the women got all teary eyed when we said our, "I do's." I kissed the bride amid cheers and applause. The love in Kate's green eyes was reflected in mine. We hadn't any doubts about our decision. Life can be very good sometimes.

We received hugs and handshakes from all when they filed past congratulating us. The music of guitars and fiddles started up behind us and the fandango was on. The smell of roasting beef was in the air. The best of life was ours today, and the looks I got from my new bride gave promise of more to come.

People danced to the music and anticipated the celebratory supper being prepared. A keg of beer and some bottles of sour mash whiskey got plenty of attention from the men and even a few of the women. I was glad to see Rooster spinning a tale to some of the cowboys, and doing it as well as ever gesturing in the air with one arm. There would be laughter and heads bobbing soon.

Charley and Cort danced and looked at each other like they were something you would put on flapjacks. It wouldn't be too many circuits before the preacher had business here again.

Kathleen was surrounded by ladies, all of whom seemed to be talking at the same time, with an occasional chorus of laughter. It was probably about their menfolk's inability to understand the simplest things all women of course instinctively knew. I reached in and pulled my new bride close.

"You can have her later, Jack. Give her to us for now," said one of the rancher's wives.

"I need to borrow her for the next dance, Bardy." I felt richer today than had I never picked up the first gold nugget from the ruins at the butte. Wealth isn't always measured in gold.

"Jack, I hope we are always this happy." Kate said.

"Sweetheart, we'll have times like this, and have each other to share the hard knocks too."

I felt a tap on my shoulder and Rooster said, "May I cut in, Cap'n? I need a little dancing practice with this sore arm before Maria drags me out here by my good one."

"Go right ahead my friend," I said and passed Kate to him. I stepped to the edge of the crowd and lighted one of the cigars Maxie had given me for a wedding present. I took a short walk away from the festivities, enjoying the day and the cigar.

As I walked my eyes scanned the horizon, seeing the valley cliffs and trees reach up for some cotton ball clouds rolling around blue skies. I was looking at nothing in particular when I saw the Indian. He was sitting at the edge of the cliff rocks, not more than a hundred yards away. If I hadn't looked straight at him I wouldn't have known of his presence. He carried no weapons, and I knew he meant me no harm. He looked familiar. The only Indians I had seen this close in months were the tame ones in Fort Stockton, and the three in the desert I threw the party for. I recognized him as Apache. All Indians don't look alike contrary to eastern belief. If he were one of those three, what was he doing here?

I raised my hand palm outward and held it in the air. A moment later he made the same gesture. There was a truce and a bond between us I didn't understand, but I knew I had nothing to fear from this warrior, nor he from me. I bent my head forward to relight my cigar. When I raised my head he was gone. I heard the sound of approaching horses. This must be what caused him to leave. It was probably late guests arriving.

I walked back to the wedding party, and met the horsemen who definitely weren't wedding guests judging from the hardware they carried and the badges on their vests. The sheriff dismounted, tipped his hat to the guests, and walked toward me.

"Captain Jack, we ain't trying to crash your wedding party, but we got some bad news you folks need to hear."

"Then speak to us straight away, sheriff. It needs to be heard or you wouldn't be here."

"I'll just spit it out. Vass Hart escaped the state prison two days ago along with Rafe Hall and Cliff Britt. They may be headed this way."

"I told them there was a rope waiting for them here if they ever returned."

"That ain't the worst part," he continued.

The look of concern on his face told me something was coming I didn't want to hear.

"Colonel "Crazy" Miller and some of his butchers escaped with him."

A cold desert wind blew across my soul with those words. My hand moved to my side, to the empty spot where my gun belt was usually tied. I saw several pairs of eyes in the crowd scanning the rocks. The sheriff's words brought back memories of a murdering fanatic who continued his bloody ways after the war was over. The atrocities he and his band of criminals had committed under the shield of war had been found inexcusable, and the continuance afterward branded him an insane butcher. If there was a way to fan the flames of hate between north and south to resurrect his reign of terror he would find it.

The wedding guests departed before dark. Unhealed war wounds were opened again by the sheriff's words. Dark clouds descended over the territory on the first day of our marriage. Damn Vass Hart and his band to hell! I posted outriders, and some of the hands had gone with the posse to search for any signs of the fugitives.

I sat under the ramada, alone with my new bride.

"Jack, who is this man everyone is afraid of? I heard mention of his name back east with disdain, but not much else."

"He is Lucifer in a Confederate uniform, a fanatic who would revive the war and a man who massacred civilians along with their children for having northern sympathies." I had met him during the war, and still had a sour taste in my mouth from it.

"Why was he imprisoned here instead of one of the prisons back east?" Kate said.

"The authorities probably thought he would have less influence among the prison population here. Like Lucifer, he attracts the worst kind of man because he condones their lawlessness."

"Will the renegades come here?"

"Vass Hart maybe. The colonel has no reason to." I thought of the gold hidden at the butte and the carnage that rabid dog would cause if it came into his hands. It was not a good thought. I decided to change the subject. I stretched my arms wide and faked a large yawn and winked at my bride.

"It's kind of early for bedtime, Jack, it is barely dark. It is so nice out here I think I could sit here all night," she said.

I turned my head to see her teasing grin, and got a bawdy wink when she arose from the chair.

"Give me about ten minutes then come to me my husband."

I did.

Chapter 21

I sat erect in the saddle with my uniform great coat buttoned and my hat squared. It prominently displayed the CSA badge on its crown. It was a hot summer day and I stared down at a man I was beginning to hate. I wasn't allowed to move and my arm was getting tired from holding my saber erect.

My horse stood stationary while I suffered the artist's brushstrokes on canvas. Kate sat behind him, smiling approvingly at his work and my discomfort. She had commissioned the painter to do family portraits, and as a new husband I wanted to make her happy. I had to admit, I enjoyed married life with all its benefits. I was happier now than I had been in years.

I spent lots of daylight on horseback patrolling the areas around Three Arrows. I looked for signs of any strangers. Perhaps the escapees had traveled out of the territory to spread their filth and meanness elsewhere, but I doubted it. Vass Hart would want his revenge on Three Arrows.

We kept our eyes open and guns loaded. I also strung a new rope with a hangman's noose tied in it on the big oak down by the river. A reminder to any uninvited visitors should they start nosing around.

"Darling," I said, "I have a ranch to look after, and my arm is falling off." I rested the saber across the saddle and started unbuttoning the great coat. The sun broke over the high cliffs and its heat was immediate.

"Alright my dear, your patience has already exceeded my expectations," said Kate.

The gentleman painting the canvas raised his head and said, "I have all I need to finish, Captain Shane. Thank you for posing as still as if I had been photographing you. I must move into the shade now to finish the background. The sun will make the colors run if I stay in it very long."

I helped him load his canvas and supplies in the wagon, then helped Katie aboard. I accompanied them to the ranch house on my horse. I hung the great coat in its customary place on the rack with my uniform hat, and lifted the saber to the mantlepiece, where it resided.

Rooster met me under the ramada, where we usually discussed the daily ranch business over coffee. We went over the usual problems about horses and cows, a minor fight in the bunkhouse, all settled now, how the crops were doing, and so forth. We had gotten to the weather and it was Rooster who got to laughing first. The same thought hit me, and I started laughing. Rooster spoke the thought aloud.

"Cap'n Jack, how many times have you seen two old graybeards sitting on the porch in rocking chairs talking about the weather like we are now?"

"Hell Rooster, we ain't even turned gray yet, well maybe a little around the ears."

"I heard something from some of the hands that might heat up your blood some. They spotted some wickiups in a canyon a few miles from here. Not sure exactly where from their description, but the hands said they looked fairly new from a distance. They weren't too keen on taking a closer look."

I studied on that for a moment then said, "I have lived most of my life near Apaches and know the country well as anyone, including them. None of them have ever lived within miles of here. I'm wondering why they're here now? Want to take a ride?" Something else I had on my mind but didn't speak of, was the fact that if you were close enough to see their wickiups, you were close enough for their lookouts to see you. You wouldn't see them unless they wanted you to. There was something happening with the Indians, and for our own protection we needed to know what it was.

From here to the border, Apaches are a part of life, as much as the coyotes or rattlesnakes or cactus. You either avoided them or dealt with them depending on their actions. They did the same. Apaches did most of their fighting with other tribes, mainly the Comanche. Occasionally, a horse or a cow went missing from a ranch, or something fired up the younger ones like the trio I ran into at the butte, but most of the time it was live and let live. A ranch with the strength of Three Arrows had little to fear.

Rooster and I saddled our horses and rode south across the country I love. I let my eyes rove over the trail, searching for any sign of Indians or the escaped prisoners. We stuck to the high ground for a better view of the land. Nothing looked interesting for the first few miles, and as always, Rooster was good company. His wounded arm had healed and served him well enough not to be a burden. He couldn't swing a rope anymore, but he didn't need to.

Around noon, we stopped to rest and water the horses at a small branch with a little shade close by. They drank their fill while we ate biscuits Maria had given Rooster that morning, along with a big kiss. I had a feeling that preacher was going to have to make regular visits to Three Arrows.

We stayed on the high ground where we could see for some distance, but that also made us visible to any lookouts or traveling parties. I hoped we saw them first if they weren't friendly.

We reached the rim of the canyon where the hands reported seeing the wickiups, and saw our Indians. From the number of braves we could see lying on the ground, they had been in a hellacious fight with someone. The wounded were bandaged in bloody rags, and a chanting shaman danced and shook a medicine pole over them. A squaw was making the rounds with a clay pot and dipper, administering water to the wounded. One of the braves had a broken arrow shaft protruding from his ribs, which meant it was other Indians who had attacked them, most likely Comanches. No love lost between the two tribes.

"Cap'n, I hate to see men hurt badly as these are, even if they are Apache," said Rooster.

"So do I, Rooster. They can't even post a lookout. They don't have a chance if the Comanches return. Chances are they just got in the way of a war party headed north. Notice anything funny about those wickiups?"

"One of them looks older from the looks of the green covering on the rest of them. It has medicine poles hanging outside, but I don't see any scalps hanging. My guess is this is the home of that shaman down there. I'm thinking the others came here for the benefit of his healing magic."

"That's what I was thinking too. We got nothing to fear here. Do you think we would miss a couple of cows?"

"If you're thinking what I think you are, I'll get the Butterfield brothers to run a couple of head over here, but not too close. They can drive them through the valley in the morning."

"That's what I'm thinking. Indians or not, these are men not able to fend for themselves. A good turn from us now will be remembered down the line."

* * *

"How would you like to be a trail boss, Cort?" I asked him. It was a decision Rooster and I had discussed, and we both knew he was the right choice. The herd was ready to market, and the railroad wasn't going to come to us. All of us sat at the breakfast table when I asked the question.

"I like it just fine right here, Captain Jack." He and Charley sat close and held hands under the table as always. Katie wasn't feeling well this morning, and she hadn't joined us yet.

"I think you are ready for it, Cort, even if you do like the scenery better at Three Arrows." I winked at Charley and she blushed.

"How long will he be gone Unka Jack?" asked Charley.

"A little over two months to Kansas and back I'd guess."

"Two months!" They both echoed with mouths left hanging open.

Charley ran out of the kitchen yelling, "Aunt Katie, Aunt Katie, it's the end of the world!"

"Two months," said Cort, sitting there with a blank look on his face.

"Rooster will go along to take care of the sales and money. You've been on a drive with him before, and know he'll back you up. Take Diego and Juan to chuck for you, a couple of wranglers to look out after the horses and as many hands as you need for riders."

"Two months," said Cort, still in his trance.

"Just a suggestion, Cort, but why don't you and Charley try to spend some time together before you leave? By the way, Indians have scalped all the hands, and are burning down the barn right now."

"Two months," he said again.

I laughed and I took my coffee outside. Nothing I could say right now was going to be heard by Cort Benner.

Rooster and I sat on the dog run and drank our coffee and chuckled about young love. He laughed and said, "This might be the fastest cattle drive to Kansas ever. Cort may stampede the herd all the way to Abilene. I hope the cowboys can keep up with them." We both laughed.

I was concerned about the escaped prisoners still at large. There had been no trace of them, except for rumors of confederate veterans being approached by strangers trying to stir up interest in resurrecting the southern cause. Such stories had been heard since the surrender, but not much stock was put in them.

We would be shorthanded for a couple of months with a dozen men gone. Enough hands would remain behind to run Three Arrows and show our presence on the ranch. Being a cautious man I didn't like so few guns protecting us, but I figured Cort needed them more on his first cattle drive as trail boss.

The day finally came to start the drive to Kansas. I rode out to the chuck wagon where the crew was gathered. I wanted to give them an incentive to spur them on to Kansas.

"Men, if I couldn't count on you to get these cows to the rail head you wouldn't be here. You might have to ride through stampedes and lightning storms, and fight Indians before you get to the end of the trail, so every cowpuncher here gets a bonus when you deliver the herd. I'm sure you boys can find some place to spend it." This brought a round of cheers and grins.

"Last drive we was on you gave us a bonus, and we brought a lot of these cows here, Cap'n."

"I did, Cort. They have gotten fat, and the herd has grown considerably. There are over two thousand head of cattle ready for market. We will make a fine profit in Kansas, and this is only our first drive. There will be many more every year until we get a rail head nearer Three Arrows. By the way boys, that bonus is a hundred dollars."

"A hundred dollars?" said one of the hands, "Let's get these cows moving north!"

Cort came over to me and asked if he could have a few words in private with me. We walked around the back of the wagons. He kind of shuffled back and forth on one foot and finally got the words to forming. I knew what was coming.

"Captain Jack, I asked Charley to marry me when we got back from the drive. Would you and Miss Kate give me your permission since her daddy's passed on?" he said.

"I think you are supposed to ask me first, but Charley is old enough now not to need my permission. Thanks for having enough respect for me to ask. Katie and I couldn't have picked a better man for her husband, Cort."

He grinned from ear to ear. "Thank you, sir."

"I'll tell Charley when I go back to the house. You had better get moving if you are going to earn that thousand dollar bonus the trail boss gets."

His eyes got big and he cupped his hands around his mouth and yelled to the riders, "Move 'em out!"

* * *

Turtle the Wise

Aieeee! I hate the Comanches. Stone Knife and Pony Stealer were badly wounded by them, and many killed. They attacked before morning light while the village slept. I had moved my wickiup closer to my Ganh several moons ago, or I would have been surprised too.

Word of my friendship with a Ganh and my healing powers have spread through the People. The wounded were brought to me and I will try to save them all. My medicine must be strong.

How will I feed them all? More will be coming and I have little food. If the Comanches find us here they will kill us all. We have no warriors strong enough to climb the rocks to watch for them. Yesterday I saw two riders at the top of the canyon. They were not Comanche and one looked like the Ganh. I knew they meant no harm. I silently asked for help for our wounded who are not all warriors. Some are boys and some are women. And they all are hungry.

* * *

If I were not a warrior I would have cried today. The white men who serve the Ganh brought us cows to the mouth of the canyon. Now my people would not starve. I know they were sent by him. We saw the sign of three arrowheads burnt into their hides. The sign of the Ganh. I will pay him a visit tonight when the moon is high.

* * *

I rode my pony through the valley close to the Ganh's wickiup. Silently, I made my way to a window. In the glow of moonlight I could see Him on the wall sitting on his horse with a long knife. That was the skin He put on to become the soldier in gray. He must have many skins to become anyone or anything, for He is a Ganh.

I left my tribute next to the door of his wickiup, and silently walked to my horse. I turned and silently thanked Him for His help again. The ride to the canyon was easy with the moon risen.

Chapter 22

"Charley, may I see the necklace you made out of those arrowheads I gave you?"

She loosened the necklace, and handed it to me. I compared it to the one found hanging on the door handle. The arrowheads were identical. I knew who our canyon guests were now. The necklace left on the door was made with three arrowheads in the shape of a turtle, some turquoise stones, and bird feathers. These arrowheads had become a bond between the Apaches at the canyon and myself. Damned if I could figure out why. I handed Charley's necklace back to her, and slipped the other necklace over my head and under my shirt.

I carried my coffee outside and sat in a chair under the ramada. I didn't like the looks of the dust cloud approaching from the far end of the valley. Several riders were headed in this direction. With so many hands gone on the cattle drive, the men that remained were all busy with the herd. Cort and the others would return any day, but right now I was alone. I strapped on my gun belt and checked my pistol loads as a precaution.

As the riders drew closer my worst fears were realized. I recognized the uniform the lead rider was wearing. Confederate! It had been a long time since I had seen a gray and butternut uniform other than my own. This could only be a man I despised. The rabid dog who made war on women and children during the war, and who would joyfully reopen the bloody wounds of war that were barely starting to heal. Colonel "Crazy" Miller! The riffraff riding with him would be part of his snake den. I was proven right on both assumptions.

The band of pond scum, thirty riders strong, came sauntering into the courtyard. Some wore pieces of old gray uniforms that had seen better days, some wore shirts and pants patched and mended many times over, and all had the watchful look of men on the run, their eyes darting from side to side and occasionally turning to look at their back trail. In the lead was the colonel and behind him was, Vass Hart! Rafe Hall and Cliff Britt followed. It was going to be a bad day for someone. Probably me.

The colonel dismounted and said, "Good morning Captain Shane. I compliment you on your ranch. No small accomplishment for a captain, even in our glorious army. I have a proposition for you. May I sit down and discuss it with you?"

"Come," I said. I needed to find out his intentions. As long as he was civil I would be too. I reminded myself the women were in the house: Kate asleep in our bedroom and Charley in the kitchen. I was as outnumbered as the defenders of the Alamo were. I didn't want the same results.

He dismounted and sat in the chair next to me. His ragtag militia remained mounted, and eyeballed everything in sight like hungry coyotes who found a rabbit hutch.

"What's on your mind, Colonel?" I asked. Under the table, I loosened the hammer strap on my holster.

"Captain Shane, I'm sure your sympathies for the southern cause are aligned with mine and our all-volunteer militia. Surrender was never an option for me. I was imprisoned to keep me from fighting for the Stars and Bars until my last breath, but prison bars will not stand between me and our righteous cause." He seemed to be staring at something above me only he could see.

"The war's over Colonel," I said. He remembered I was

sitting there, and stared at me with a look in his eyes like a bull ready to stampede if you were obliging enough to open the gate.

"Only because we didn't have the required financing and manufacturing, Captain." He looked over the table at me with what may have been the start of a grin and said, "The opportunity for you to become part of this dream is at hand, Captain! At hand!"

Whenever someone mentions my name and the word opportunity in the same sentence I tend to watch my back. When a raging madman does it I want my gun in my hand. It was there now under the table.

"It has come to my attention you may have acquired some spoils of war in the form of a large amount of gold. The only currency with any monetary value since the war. I know you want to see our proud flag flying again." He looked again at that vision in the sky, gesturing with his arms pointed towards his imagined heavens.

"First, here in New Mexico territory, then Texas, then state by state, marching across the south with our numbers constantly growing until we take the entire Confederate nation back. Then perhaps the northern states, then Canada and Mexico. We would then be strong enough to march around the globe if we so desired." He paused, and looked down at me face to face.

"There is a place at the top for you, Captain. It is time I become general over this army and I need an experienced officer such as you as my second in command. Truthfully, how does Colonel Shane sound to you?"

I grinned at him and said, "To be truthful, mister Miller, I think you are one crazy son of a bitch," and stuck the barrel of my gun in his ear.

"Vass," I shouted, "you and Rafe and Cliff will save me a lot of trouble by taking a ride down to the big oak tree with the hangman's nooses hanging, and put your head in one. I told you they would be waiting for you if you came back. Your friends know the way." Rafe and Cliff's horses seemed to be a little restless. There was a scowl on Hart's ugly face.

"Cap'n Jack, that gun ain't pointed at me, and there are twenty-eight of us sitting here armed and dangerous like. You sure you don't want to be more hospitable to your old friends?" said Hart.

"I meant what I said...coward!" I spit the last word out to take a jab at him in front of his friends. I could tell by the red leaking into his face it had worked. I might as well keep it up.

"It's bad enough you scaring all the women and children in the territory with that face, and attracting he-skunks with that stripe down your back, jailbird." His fuse was lit for sure now. His hand started inching towards his holster. If I could get him to draw it would be no contest with my gun already in my hand. Even the outlaws he rode with have their idea of self-defense being a fair fight between two men.

I said, "I may even tell them your secret, Vass."

Whatever that secret is, it affected him as though I held him over a cliff. His gun hand froze. There was fear and hate in his eyes. He wanted to skin me slowly, and I didn't know why.

And then the situation changed. Two of the outlaws came around the side of the ranch house dragging Charley by each arm. They wrestled her over to Hart's horse and he lifted her up on the saddle. The fear I had seen before, turned into an evil smugness with her as a shield. Charley's eyes had teared up, but I knew her temper was rising by the second.

"Looks like I got me some trade goods now, Cap'n," Hart sneered.

"So do I," I said and cocked the hammer on the pistol I held against the Colonel's head.

Vass pulled his knife and pretended to sharpen it on his saddle. He raised it to Charley's neck and grinned at me. A look of surprise replaced his grin. He touched his left ear and brought back a bloody hand. He stared at it with a puzzled look, and his right ear disappeared as a clap of thunder was heard, followed by another. It was my turn to grin now. I recognized the sound of that thunder...Cort Benner's widow maker sniper rifle. Nobody, but him could have shot the ears off a man from the distance that thunder traveled. The Three Arrows hands had returned from the cattle drive.

Panic ensued among the outlaws. Rafe Hall and Cliff Britt were galloping away in the opposite direction. They wanted as much distance as possible between themselves and the nooses waiting for them here. The rest of the riders decided they no longer liked the odds either and followed suit.

Hart appeared to be in shock. His hands held his head on each side. Charley slid off the horse and picked up the knife he had dropped. Vass turned his horse with his knees to gallop away.

Charley yelled, "Don't forget this," and stuck the knife in his backside. With a roar of pain he tore out of the courtyard, alternating between curses and yells. I sat with my gun held on my prisoner and laughed until I had tears in my eyes.

Minutes later, Cort, Rooster, and the rest of the hands rode into the yard. Cort still held his rifle. He got off his horse and ran to Charley. They immediately tied themselves in a knot of arms and lips.

"Nice shooting, Cort," I said.

"Thanks, Cap'n Jack, I would have got him dead center, but Charley was in the way."

Rooster said, "I reckon someone's friends are going to have to speak a little louder to him from now on."

One of the hands added, "At least he won't have to listen to any of your stories!"

Rooster laughed along with the rest of us. The men loved his stories, even if he did take a few liberties with the truth now and then. Rooster could read an almanac and have you laughing.

"Is this who I think it is?" asked Rooster.

"Yep, the one and only Colonel "Crazy" Miller, I said.

Since I had held my gun to his head, he hadn't moved or spoken. He did now.

"Captain Shane, you have been remarkable, standing off the whole militia single-handed. I have to ask you a question if I may."

"Go ahead."

"Simply, why did you choose to fight for the south, when all of your interests are here in New Mexico, and you didn't own any slaves? Please humor me and explain your position."

"Not much to explain. Most people said the war was fought to free the slaves, but never gave much thought to the fact there wasn't one out of a thousand confederate soldiers who ever owned one. Most of us didn't believe it was right anyway. We fought Comanches and the Mexican army right here. We furnished everything we needed with our own sweat and lots of blood. There is a cemetery under those cottonwoods by the river," I said, and pointed towards the trees, "where my first wife, brother, and sister in law are buried. During this fighting and carving out a life for ourselves, there was no federal government present to fire a shot in our defense or put food in our pots. Our family came to this country and fought against the British for the same thing the federal government was doing to the south by taxing it and making laws they had to obey with little or no regard for their rights. As a territory, we don't even have state's rights which is the real reason the war was fought. I fought for our freedom and independence. It's that simple."

I had two of the hands tie up the colonel and throw him in the back of a wagon to deliver him to the sheriff. He would soon be back behind those prison bars standing between him and his righteous cause. Now all I had to worry about was the renegades from hell he had assembled.

Chapter 23

I had to return to the butte and hide the gold. This incident convinced me of the potential evil it could buy in the wrong hands. How and where I was going to hide it were questions I didn't have the answers for yet.

Colonel "Crazy" Miller was now safely back in a cage, where his hate and insanity were contained. I hated to think what might have happened, if the Three Arrows hands hadn't returned when they did. I would have paid any price for Charley's safety.

Unfortunately, Vass Hart and the rest of those outhouse droppings had gotten away. The last we had seen of them was the dust cloud left behind at the other end of the valley.

Katie had missed everything. She was feeling poorly, and spent much of her time in bed. I had sent for the sawbones in town, and he would be here today. I was smart enough to make no attempt at understanding female maladies. For some reason, Katie became frustrated with what she called, "your total ignorance of the adult female." I hoped there was a cure for whatever she had. She was temperamental most days, and I was spending a lot more time with the cows.

Cort and Charley had gotten married. Friends and neighbors attended in abundance, and it was a wingding as big as Katie's and mine had been. Every Three Arrows man and woman helped mix the adobe and lay the stones to build a house for the newlyweds. The first month they were married, Rooster and the hands joked with Cort about how poorly he looked every morning, and offered to let him bunk with the hands if he thought he could sleep better. Cort would smile and shake his head. Charley would blush and run if she were in the vicinity.

The Apache village in the box canyon had several wickiups built now, but we never saw the Indians outside of their canyon. Their wounded were healing, and they seemed to be grateful for the safety of Three Arrows and the steers I sent them occasionally. They never killed one of the herd. I hoped we stayed peaceful.

"Cap'n Jack, there's a couple of ladies looking for you."

I turned to see Rooster riding up behind me. I had ridden to the top of a rise where a small stand of pines overlooked the valley. I enjoyed the smell of the pine needles and the sound of the wind blowing across the valley meadow below. It was a good place to get away from things and catch up on my thinking. Rooster knew where to look for me.

"Collecting my thoughts, Rooster."

"Where'd they get scattered to?" he said, and chuckled at his humor.

"All over the New Mexico territory and Texas too."

"Well if ya can get 'em back in your head from all them places, Miss Kate wants to see her one and only back at the ranch house. Doc Kari is there waiting too."

"Something wrong, Rooster? I never heard of this sawbones before."

"Something's up, but they ain't confided in me, Cap'n, and you're gonna have a surprise when you meet this doc. I reckon we ought to get down there pretty soon."

We pointed our horses towards home, and rode at a light gallop all the way. I wasn't sure what I was riding into, but if a sawbones was there, it was important.

We reached the ranch house, and tied our horses to the

hitching rail. Katie and Charley sat on the porch, in the shade, with an unfamiliar female. All the families in the territory enjoyed the visit of females. There weren't many, and the ones there soon became friends. Women need other women's company in a way men will never understand, according to Katie.

I smiled and lifted my hand in greeting. "Hello neighbor, good to see another lady in our home. I know Katie and Charley appreciate your visit, and I hope they invited you to stay for supper."

She smiled back and said, "You must be Captain Jack. Your lovely bride and niece are telling me all about you. As much as I enjoy your family, I'm here on a professional visit."

Katie grinned and said, "Meet Doctor Melissa Kari. She is assisting old Doc Conger with some of his house calls."

I have no problem with female doctors. I remembered them in field hospitals during the war. I had seen them covered in blood, sleepless for days, while an endless procession of wounded men were brought to them. They had saved thousands of lives on both sides.

"Charley has some news for you, Jack," Katie said, and exchanged glances with Charley.

"You're going to have a great nephew this spring, Unka Jack!" Charley blurted out.

"Hooray! We can always use another cowboy around here," I said.

"How about two cowboys, Papa?" Katie said patting her stomach, and her green eyes said the rest.

* * *

Winter rode in hard and mean, and was stubborn as a Missouri mule leaving. We lost numerous head of cattle in the frigid cold and deep snow in spite of all our efforts. Three Arrows had been snowbound from the rest of the territory for weeks, but now the snow was turning into small streams feeding the bigger ones all the way into the Pecos. Soon the grass would start to green out, and make fat cows out of skinny ones. Next year we would have abundant feed from our farms.

Vass Hart had been seen far south of here, around the Mexican border. It was reported he had killed a man in a saloon fight, who had commented on his ears, or lack of. He would return one day, and I intend to make good on my promise to hang him.

A cavalry detachment from Fort Stockton came to warn the area ranches of possible Comanche raids this spring. Quanah Parker and his band had jumped the reservation along with several others. They were hundreds of miles north, and I hoped they stayed there until the army could get them under control. We were lucky that raiding party passed us by when they hit the Apache camp last year.

Katie and Charley looked and acted like expectant mothers. They alternated between bawling for no reason to snapping mine and Cort's heads off. In self-defense, we had braved the foul weather many times, using the herd as an excuse to steal away to a nice peaceful blizzard. This morning I was in the barn shoeing an ornery roan horse. He would only kick and bite me.

I had formed a plan for the gold hidden on top of the butte. I was still working out the details, but it was doable. I would depart with the cattle drive in case the ranch was watched. I had to ensure no one followed me, and the rest I would have to do alone.

My thoughts were interrupted by Juan Mancha's frantic voice. "*Capitano* Jack! *Senora* Charley is time!" I hammered the last nail in the roan's shoe, and followed Juan back to the Benner house. Rooster was outside boiling water over a cook fire. The women were assembled and defending the bedroom like it was a water hole in the desert. I could hear Charley yelling out her pain at Cort, "Cortright Benner, don't you ever touch me again! If you loved me you wouldn't make me hurt this much. I hate you!"

A distraught, soon to be father was outside pacing the dog run, looking like he had lost his last friend. I figured it was safest to head in his direction.

"Cap'n Jack, why is she hating me, is she going to die, is she hurting that much, is she going to be O.K. or is she gonna die or..."

"Whoa, cowboy. Women been having babies since Adam and Eve, and it's never easy, but she's going to be just fine," I said.

"Really?"

"Really."

"Whew, I was pretty worried. I never been around any birthings before. Can I ask you something, Cap'n?"

"Sure, Cort."

"Do you think she really meant that part about me never touching her again?"

Chapter 29

The chuck and two other wagons were packed with supplies, the wranglers were walking spare mounts, and the cattle herd started the slow move to market. The outriders coaxed reluctant strays back to the herd, while several of the larger steers were jostling each other for the lead position. The cows were kicking up dust and this year's cattle drive was started.

I told Cort I would ride with him for a day or so to help start the drive. The real reason of course, was that I didn't want to be seen leaving the ranch alone and followed. I had felt I was being watched on several occasions since the snows had left. Whether by white men or Indians, or both, I couldn't say, but I knew they were there. My plans were risky enough without any interference. I could use help, but that would mean burdening someone else with the secret of the gold. It was too much to load a man down with.

Rooster, stayed at the ranch to look after the women and our new addition, Austin Shane Benner. Yes, I was proud of his name. I hired a few more hands knowing we would be shorthanded during the drive, and a few extra guns around might come in handy if there was any trouble. Kate was suffering during her pregnancy, and her time would be soon. This was another reason for me to hurry and get this thing done. I kissed her goodbye, and hoped the weary look in her eyes would be gone when I returned.

We stopped the herd in late afternoon at a small stream. We had made about ten miles, and everyone had settled into their duties. Juan had the chuck stove cooking beans in a cast iron pot, and beef steaks frying in a large skillet next to it. I asked him to put together some biscuits and side meat to take with me. It was a good meal followed by coffee and conversation around the campfire with the cowboys. I listened to outrageous stories and lies and laughs. If Rooster had been there he would have trumped them all. I said goodnight to Cort and the hands and broke out my bedroll.

Before daylight I stirred up the campfire coals and made a pot of coffee. I was enjoying a cup of it when Cort rode up. He had already checked on the night riders and the herd. He was a good trail boss.

"Morning Cap'n."

"Morning Cort. Different from your first drive last year isn't it?" I said.

He smiled, "Yep, you could say that."

"Do you still miss Charley as much, Cort?"

"Yep, and Austin too," he answered with a smile on his face.

"Glad to hear it. A lot of men look forward to getting away from their wives even if it means they are going to fight Comanches."

"I know it ain't that way with you and Miss Kate, but there was a fellow in the war with me who said it was more peaceable at Chickamauga than at home with his missus."

"Guess we're the lucky ones, Cort, we only have to contend with them being like that when they are in a family way. We are lucky we both didn't get frostbite last winter." We chuckled at the memory.

"Cap'n, can I ask you something?"

"Sure, Cort."

"You didn't need to come this far with us. You know the boys and me can handle ourselves and the herd. Is everything all right with the ranch?"

You couldn't slip much by, Cort. I had to tell him some of it. "Men like Vass Hart and his bunch will always be out there looking for a chance to take down Three Arrows. The only reason they can't is because we are stronger than they are. I needed to leave the ranch with the drive in case I was being watched. There are some things I have to do, and I have to do them alone. Once I am finished Three Arrows and the territory around us will be safer than ever before. I'm sorry, Cort, but I can't tell you any more than that."

"Can I help?" he asked.

"I'm counting on you to look out for this drive and our hands. That's more than enough to keep your hands full." I shook hands with him, and mounted my horse.

I rode east toward the first streaks of dawn. It was a dark gray morning with the promise of a storm. Two days later I rode into Comanche territory.

* * *

I sat quiet in the rocks watching the Comanche raiding party pass. They moved from the direction of the border, driving stolen horses and Mexican captives who would be sold to Comancheros, if they lived that long. Not wanting to join their ranks I kept my head down and my horse gentled. They were a large party. Their dust and the wind would wipe out the tracks I had made this morning. A lone rider wouldn't interest this party, they were looking for bigger game. I didn't like the direction they were headed toward settled territory. They had already taken a brother from me, and I had a lot more to lose now. I was glad I had hired the additional hands at Three Arrows.

Midland was a welcome sight when I arrived. I was covered in dust, but my scalp was intact. I left my horse at the livery stable, and went looking for a room. I found a hotel close by and requested bath water be drawn. Washing off a few layers of dust appealed to me more than the room and bed did. I'd as soon spread my bedroll in the livery, but I wasn't partial to bathing in horse troughs.

I sent the desk clerk out for a bottle of sour mash, and climbed in the tub of hot water. He returned with the bottle, and I sampled it before dismissing him with a good tip. It was the good stuff I requested. Not some homemade coyote piss a saloon was trying to pass off as sipping whiskey.

While the prairie dust dissolved, I mentally went over my checklist of supplies awaiting me; a wood stove, blacksmith tools, bellows, a half ton of coal, food and feed for me, and two teams of mules, paint, water barrels, some sheet iron, bar stock, shovels and a bank safe. I hoped I hadn't forgotten anything.

The hotel had a dining room and an excellent cook. It was crowded. That is usually a sign of good food. Town folk and cowboys kept the kitchen busy tonight. One of the cowboys dining alone looked familiar. He was probably someone I had seen in another town or on the trail. I didn't want company, so I didn't pursue it. I ate a steak and potatoes with fresh baked bread and butter on the side. I washed it down with coffee. It was a good place to eat. As I was leaving, the cowboy from the dining room bumped into me.

"Sorry, gent," he said and continued on his way.

"No problem," I said and went out the door. I walked back to the hotel and went to bed.

I ate breakfast before daylight in the hotel's dining room. The food was as good as supper had been last night. I stuffed myself with side meat, fried eggs, and biscuits drowned in gravy. I drank a second cup of coffee, and walked to the freight yard. Streaks of orange and red were appearing in the east. I smiled at my good fortune. I knew what those colors meant.

The freight yard office was already open and occupied by an

old man with the scarred face of a fighter and long white hair. Judging from his appearance, he had been down more than one rocky road in his life.

"Good morning, are you the owner?" I asked.

"Looks like some rain coming in from the looks of that sky. Yep, this paradise is all mine." He waved his hand over his couple of acres of wood fences, freight wagons and stables. All of which had seen their best days, but still clean and serviceable. I had a feeling he ran a tight operation.

He looked up at me and said, "You wouldn't happen to be Jack Shane would you?"

"I just might, what's your name friend?"

"Folks call me Strange Bill. That's because of all the strange things freighted through here, and yours didn't help that reputation none. That war surplus freight wagon you had delivered puts all mine to shame. The wheels are taller than a tall man and over a foot wider than a long foot. I barely rounded up enough mules to pull it. There was some interest in that bank safe too. I had to leave the door open so nobody would get a notion there was any money in it."

"That freight wagon is the only way I can move the safe north to a new bank that is being built. I had plenty of room in the bed for the blacksmith's supplies, and a wood stove too," I lied.

"It's a big'un alright. If you're ready to pull out I'll have Pancho and his boys hitch up the mules and load the supplies. A word of caution if you're headed north. The Comanches are raiding again, and outlaws have robbed travelers on the main road. Watch your hair and your poke."

"I aim to," I said.

I had the wagon wheels rolling north in less than an hour. The ruts those big wheels left behind would lead anyone straight to me, so I kept a northern course until the rain came in from the east. When it came down hard I threw on my slicker and turned into it, confidant it would wash away my tracks. I pointed the mules in the direction of the butte...and the gold.

* * *

It felt good to have a hammer in my hand again. Blacksmithing is a way of life on a ranch, where you have to do your own shoeing and metal work if you want it done. My father taught me well, as his father taught him, and I enjoyed making the metal yield to my will. I had constructed a forge in the small canyon wall the second day after my arrival at the butte. I had made a simple and functional work area to serve my needs.

On the drive here from Midland, I had changed directions several times, using the weather to cover my tracks. If the Comanche war party found those tracks I would go under for certain, or wish I had if I was captured.

My horse and the mules were grazing in the new grass and drinking from the small pond. I had worried about the abundance of both of these, but spring had been generous. After unloading the wagon with the help of the freight boom and windlass, I set up my workbench on the wagon's tail gate. I would sleep in the wagon and cook on the wood stove until it was time to take it apart, piece by piece.

Everything was as I had left it. The jars were still filled with the gold that had been there hundreds of years. It would have taken me several days to carry it all down from the storage rooms in the upper part of the butte, but fortunately there was a landing above the canyon where I could drop it straight down, a little at a time.

It took a couple of days to transfer the gold, and now I had at least a week of hot and heavy work in front of me, before I could head back to Three Arrows. How I was going to avoid the Comanche war party and bandits on the return trip weighed heavily on my mind. It would take some luck to dodge them on the home trail. I had a couple of ideas up my sleeve that might help.

The bank safe lay on the ground where I had rolled it off the wagon. Once I removed the locking mechanisms I would have to dig a hole next to it and bury it. I would have to do the same with the wood stove.

Every day felt more strenuous than the previous one. I was exhausted and needed rest, but there was no time. I had built molds, and formed others in the ground to make the pieces I required. I built a fire in the forge each morning and fed it until I could do no more each night. It took me a week to shape and pour all the pieces.

Using the freight boom, I raised each piece I had made to the wagon, and assembled them after much fitting, filing, and drilling. I polished the surfaces to a smooth finish and gave everything two coats of paint, inside and out. When finished, I stood back admiring my handiwork. Not a bad 'smithing job at all, my father would have been proud.

I stripped off my work clothes, walked to the pond, and sat down in the deep end with only my head sticking out of the water. The coolness felt good to my hot and tired body. I scraped off some of the black with a scrub brush. Feeling refreshed, I made a pot of coffee and fried the last of my side meat with a potato and some dried chili peppers. Not bad fare for the trail. I ate my supper and poured myself a half cup of coffee.

I uncorked the sour mash jug and filled the rest of the coffee cup with my daily reward. I made the long hike up the stone stairway to the top of the butte. I sat on a rock and looked in all directions for sign of a campfire or company. As usual, there was none. It was late evening and the last brushstrokes of sunset were slowly fading. The sour mash coffee tasted good and I listened to the north wind play a musical symphony heard only in the desert at night.

I spent the next day preparing for the trip back to Three Arrows. It was too late in the season to count on rain to cover the wagon tracks. Worrying about those tracks leading to me would do no good. I put those thoughts aside, and started making the canyon appear as it did when I arrived. I buried the remaining tons of gold I didn't have room for on the wagon, at the bottom of the hole I had dug for the wood stove. I dug the hole next to the stove then dug under the side of the hole until the stove fell into it. I did the same in another hole with the safe. I have a lot more respect for miners and gravediggers now than I did a week ago.

As I had previously done, I blocked in the rock staircase behind the prickly pear and cholla cactus, and pulled the cactus that hid it back in place. By late afternoon, I had removed the other signs of my presence in the canyon. I rolled out my bedroll and grabbed myself some shuteye.

I awakened at twilight. I saddled my horse and hitched up the mule teams. It was time to leave the canyon and head to Three Arrows. I planned to travel at night as much as I could. I knew the country well, and most of it was flat. I was counting on luck to get me most of the way. This was a vast area, mostly unpopulated by white men or Indian. My chances were good except for those wagon tracks behind me. They were as good as a treasure map leading straight to me.

After traveling a quarter of a mile I pointed the freight wagon north and stopped. I walked back to the canyon brushing out the wheel track on one side with a broom, then returned to brush out the other one. It would appear I was headed north bypassing the butte. An Indian might be able to read those tracks, but a white man couldn't.

For three days I traveled after dark, sticking to the rockiest ground I could see. Before dawn, I would pull the wagon behind some rocks, or into an arroyo where it couldn't be seen. I walked the mules next to my horse for at least half a mile to any water or shelter I could find for them and myself. Without those mules, no one was taking that wagon anywhere. I brushed out their tracks around the wagon, and had a cold camp. I didn't want to risk a small cook fire being seen or smelled. I was going to take up a couple of belt notches by the time I got home. I awakened in the early afternoon, and rode down to check on the wagon. I heard voices as I got close, and pulled back on the reins. I dismounted and walked my horse back to camp, and tied him to his picket pin. Grabbing my saddle gun out of the scabbard, I worked my way back through the brush to the wagon. Hid behind a mesquite bush, I rose up enough to get a look at where the voices were coming from. My worst fears had come to pass. The voice belonged to Vass Hart! He was standing in the wagon.

* * *

Vass Hart

I may be the ugliest son of a bitch in the territory, but as soon as we get the safe open I'll be the richest one too. A smart fellow like me can make his own way in life when he gets a break this big, providing his luck doesn't go sour again. From now on it's gonna be "Mister" Hart when you're talking to me. I might even put a "Major" or "Colonel" in front of it just to outrank that bastard, Captain Jack Shane. He might as well fold this hand, because I got his safe full of Confederate gold and his freight wagon to pull it with as soon as we round up some mules. He can keep the wood stove for his trouble. Damn I cain't stop laughing.

Things were about to get away from me when we lost Colonel Miller. The boys wanted to make quick tracks over the border, and drift on down to Chihuahua. The peon in the cantina who laughed at my face did me a favor. When I shot him dead in front of them, it flat got their attention. He didn't have a gun, but that was his bad luck. I reckon the boys figured it might be safer to do things my way rather than cross me.

When Rico spotted Captain Jack in a Midland hotel he followed him to the freight yard. He saw them loading this bank safe and wood stove on one of those giant freight wagons they used in the war. He said there was a bunch of supplies loaded too. I didn't care about no wood stove or supplies, but that bank safe was made for only one thing, and I aimed to have it no matter who I had to kill.

Rico had ridden his horse into the ground to bring us the news. By the time he reached Midland, Captain Jack and his wagon had a four day head start on us. The damned rain had washed his wagon tracks out, but some cowboys told us they had seen him headed north toward Comanche country. Damn if that Captain Jack weren't slick! He'd let the Comanches guard that gold for him!

We worked our way north, but never could pick up those wagon wheel tracks. Some of the boys were nervous being deep in Indian territory, so I moved our search area in the direction of the New Mexico territories. He had to travel that country sooner or later with that safe full of gold.

We covered hundreds of miles before this glorious morning when we cut those tracks. It's hard to know how old tracks are in the desert unless you're an Indian, so we put the spurs to our horses and followed them at a good pace. I knew the wagon hadn't passed too long ago when we spotted some mule droppings. Before long, I saw the wagon in the distance and I could tell something weren't right. As we rode up we didn't see nothing moving and heard nary a sound but the wind. No sign of life. The Comanches must have sent Captain Shane under, and stole his mules. Much as I hated the bastard, I wouldn't wish on him what they probably did before they killed him, but that was his bad luck.

I looked down at Rafe working on the safe dial from the top of the safe where I was standing. After a few spins he looked puzzled and pulled the safe handle. The door swung open stiffly and he started cursing.

"What's wrong? Is it more than we can carry?" I said.

"A damned grasshopper could carry all the gold in this safe. It's empty," said Rafe.

I've never been so damned mad in my life as I am right now. Instead of all the gold I could carry, I had a wood stove and an empty safe, in the middle of the desert. I wouldn't give you two cents for everything in this wagon! The Indians must have caught Captain Jack before he could reach the gold.

I pulled my gun. I wanted to shoot something or somebody. I turned to find a target, and a gust of wind hit me in the face. There was a dust storm on the horizon. A Comanche war party at least twice our size led the storm and came toward us full gallop. I can hear their war cries. I jumped from the top of the safe to the wagon bed, then on to my horse. He ran like he was as scared of those Comanches as me.

In less than a minute I've gone from being the richest man in the territory, to running for my life. My luck has gone sour again. Damn you, Captain Jack!

* * *

I hear gunshots and war cries, but can see little in the dust storm. The sounds of battle and men's screams chill me to the bone, and memories I want to stay buried are back. I have my long gun at the ready: a bullet chambered and hammer cocked. The storm surrounded me now, and I burrowed deep into the sand under a thicket of mesquite bushes. I hear the skirmish moving away from me, but I'm going to sit tight until the only sound is the blowing of the wind. I've got a grip on the ground like a heavy frost, and as long as I'm still, I won't be found by the Indians.

Through a fog of dust, I can see a couple of warriors stop to inspect the wagon, but seeing nothing of interest in the safe or wood stove they rode to join the pursuit. Under normal circumstances they would have set fire to the wagon on general principles, but the wind was too strong, and there were scalps to be had.

It was dark when the wind stopped blowing and the night was silent. I stood up, shook the sand off, and walked to my horse and mules. They had fared well in the storm as animals usually do, and were ready for another day. Folks could learn a lot from them.

I'll hitch up the wagon before dawn and be ready to roll out at first light. It was now safe to travel during daylight since the outlaws and Indians had passed, and I will make better time by doing so. The sight of the Comanche raiding party gave me a sick feeling in my gut. I had seen what they did to people. It was time to get back home at Three Arrows and the woman I love, as fast as I can get there.

Chapter 25

Rooster

I see a rider galloping up the valley toward the ranch house. He's rawhiding his horse in an effort to outrun the Indians on his tail. He's almost inside the courtyard, but won't make it because an Indian bullet hit his horse, and took it out from under him. He's on his feet taking aim with his rifle, and he's standing there as cool as if he were target shooting, and taking an Indian down with every shot. They are almost upon him, but I can't abandon my post here on the ranch house porch to help him. The only man between those savages and the women and baby inside the house is me! All the hands are at the barn raising at the other end of the valley, and I doubt they can hear the gunshots from that distance. I'm all alone, and I don't know if I can do what has to be done when the Indians reach the houses.

I've never seen a fighter as fierce as this rider. A pistol flashing in his hand is dropping more Indians. A gunshot wound made him flinch, and it was followed by arrows to his chest and leg. When the pistol was empty, he smashed an Indian in the mouth with the gun butt. He broke off the arrow sticking out of his leg, and stabbed another attacker in the neck with the shaft. Red bodies are taking him down, and covering him like ants on an anthill. All of them trying to stab or tomahawk the poor devil. I fired both barrels of my shotgun into the pile. It's all I can do for him.

Arrows are flying at me so I better retreat while I can. I have my pistol, and now my back is to the ranch house door. Another wave of Indians are rushing toward the courtyard now. We are all going under. I will have to go inside the house when they get closer, and do for the women and baby. I will try to get to Maria after that. I hear fighting at her house now. If I'm lucky, I'll have a bullet left for myself.

* * *

Captain Jack

I can hear Katie's screams inside the ranch house. I had seen smoke rising as I was bringing the wagon up the valley, and immediately abandoned it and the mules in favor of my horse. When I got close to the house, I saw the barn smoldering and dead Indians everywhere. A white man I didn't know lay in the courtyard with an arrow sticking out of his chest. Something didn't look right, but the only thing on my mind was Kate's screams.

I reigned in hard and jumped off my horse, gun in hand. I rushed through the ranch house door and a bullet slammed into the jamb next to my head. I raised my Colt and almost shot Maria.

"*Patron*! I thought you were one of those *diablos*!" she said, and lowered the rifle she held.

"Where is Kate, what's wrong?" I yelled.

"She is fine, *Patron*."

"Is she hurt? I heard her scream."

"She is in pain like every *madre* having a *bebe.*"

I started for the bedroom door and Maria planted her open palm right in the center of my chest stopping me. I understood. I'd be in the women's way. Maybe I could boil water or something.

"*Patron, mi gallo* is in a bad way. Please go to him now. I will come for you when it is time," she said.

"Where is Rooster? Is he wounded or hurt?" I said.

"He is sitting in the rocks above the house standing guard with his rifle. He is hurt, *Patron*, but his hurt is on the inside. He did not think we would survive this attack."

The implications of this, and what Rooster's role would have been sank in. I nodded and walked out of the house. On my way to the rocks I stopped by the storehouse to pick up something we would need. It was a short climb to where I found Rooster bent over, his head in his hands. He was sobbing, and his whole body shook with emotion. I put my hand on his shoulder, and handed him the bottle of sour mash I had brought. He took it, raised it to his lips, and had a long pull from it.

"I don't know if I could have done it either, my friend," I said.

"Thanks, Cap'n. No man should be put in that spot. I was hoping to have the last bullet for myself. And not to save me from the Comanches, but because I couldn't live with myself after doing what had to be done. Everything happened pretty fast, and it's wilder than any yarn I ever spun. And I've spun some good ones."

"That you have. Who is the dead cowboy in the courtyard?"

"The toughest son of a bitch who ever lived, Cap'n. He must have killed a dozen or more by himself. He came hightailing it down the valley, probably to warn us, and that swarm of red hornets was right on his tail. You ain't going to believe what happened next."

He handed the whiskey bottle back to me. I took a drink while Rooster related the events.

"When that fellow's guns were empty he got covered up in Indians, like ants pouring out of an ant hill. I fired both loads from a double barrel into the pile, and I backed up to the door with my pistol, aiming to go inside and..." He trailed off and reached for the bottle. I passed it to him, and after he drank, motioned for him to continue.

"All of a sudden, there were more Indians coming. They were everywhere, Cap'n, I knew it was over for all of us then, but the ones riding in started fighting the ones already here. They were Apaches, not Comanches, and who knows why Indians do anything, but I think they were paying them back for that raid on their village. They couldn't have picked a better time," said Rooster.

Now I knew what was wrong when I rode up. Those dead Indians had been scalped.

"Cap'n Jack, this is fine sipping whiskey, and I've had more than a few sips now, but I swear I seen that dead man's leg move. We better climb down off these rocks and see. We owe him a debt. If he hadn't slowed those Comanches down they would have done for us before the Apaches did for them."

We eased down the rocks toward the pile of bodies and saw him move again. We hurried the rest of the way down, and pulled the dead Indians off him. He opened two blue eyes. He was alive.

"Can you talk?" I asked.

He nodded, and closed his eyes again.

"Can you take care of my horse? I know he was shot and don't want him to suffer if he ain't dead," he said.

"He's not suffering anymore," I said.

"Thanks, when you fellows bury me, please pull these damn

arrows out. Don't want to go under that way."

"Be glad to, it's the least we can do for you. What's your name, friend?" I asked.

"Cold, Martin Cold."

"The lawman?"

"Yep."

Rooster exchanged glances with me. We had both heard of Martin Cold, the legendary lawman known as "The Iceman." His moniker easily tying in with his reported demeanor in a gunfight of which there had been many. If it came to guns you wanted him on your side of the argument. I looked him over good, and didn't like what I saw. This man was seriously wounded.

"I'm going to tell it to you straight, Martin. I'm going to thank you now for what you did holding those Comanches off, because you might not be here a few minutes from now. It doesn't look good for you, but if you are the fighter I hear you are, you might make it. I got to get those arrow shafts and bullet out of you, and clean those knife and tomahawk wounds. That, and sewing you up is going to smart something fierce, but it's got to be done, or you'll go under for sure. I'll send for the doctor at Lincoln, and they'll be here in two days or less if you can hang on," I said.

"I'll do my best. You wouldn't mind sharing a drink out of that bottle would you?"

He had sand alright. This was a man to ride with. We carried him inside Rooster's room and handed him the bottle.

"If you want more, I got plenty." I said.

"This is mighty fine sour mash," he said, and took another long pull out of the bottle.

"You could have dropped in sociable like for a drink of it, Martin. No need to bring all your friends," said Rooster.

"I'll do just that next time," Martin said, and passed out either from the whiskey or loss of blood. Rooster and I sterilized our knives over the lantern flame and did what had to be done.

It was a long afternoon for Martin Cold and the two of us. After it was over, Rooster and I washed up, and sat on the ramada with a new bottle of sour mash. We had earned it today.

"Cap'n Jack, I told Juan when he went to fetch that lady sawbones to get word to the preacher to stop by here soon as he could."

"I hope it doesn't come to pass, but it's a good idea having him come to speak over Martin if he doesn't make it," I said.

"Nope, Cap'n Jack, it's marrying not burying I got on my mind. I aim to be a married man. When this fracas was going on, my heart was hurting. I was thinking what might happen to Maria if I didn't get to the Mancha's house in time. I ran there as soon as I could, and found that giant Mexican friend of ours, Diego, had been making kindling out of Comanches. They were unlucky enough to have caught him chopping firewood, and tomahawks against a double bladed wood axe in his big hands ain't a much of a fight. I made a promise to myself if we got through this, I wanted Maria next to me from now on. She ran to me with tears in her eyes. She was thinking the same thing about me. I asked her to marry me."

"What did she say?"

He smiled and said, "She said *Si!*"

I shook his hand. They would be a good pair.

The cowhands had returned from the barn raising and were wide eyed at the carnage in the courtyard. They didn't have to ask to know it had been damned close. I had them start digging a mass grave about a hundred yards from our family cemetery. I sent a couple more hands to drive the mules and wagon to the blacksmith shop. I told them to unhitch the mule teams and leave the wagon and supplies covered with tarps to be unloaded later. I didn't want them seeing what was under those tarps.

"Are you worried about Miss Kate, Cap'n?" asked Rooster.

"She's a healthy woman, and women have been having

babies since the beginning of time, but she's been in labor a long time, Rooster. Yep, it's a mite worrisome," I said.

"Maria is with her. She has lots of experience in birthing. I wouldn't worry too much."

"We are too far from civilization. We have to guard against bandits, renegades, Comanches, and those are just the big things. We got no doctor close by, no banks, no dry goods stores, and even Maxie has to make rounds for us to be able to buy the women a new dress. We have no law to protect us except ourselves, and no U.S. Army protection. One day, our children will need a school. We are only as safe as Three Arrows is strong. It's time to change all that. I've been studying on it and..." before I could finish, I heard a familiar voice.

"Unka Jack, it's a boy!" Charley yelled from the house, "Come take a look at the little critter. He sure is pretty. Oh, and Aunt Katie wants to see you too."

I took off for the house with a grinning Rooster in tow. Katie was propped up in bed holding the prettiest baby I had ever seen. She was all smiles, and he was bawling like a new calf.

"Meet your son, Garrett Shane," she said, and handed him to me.

Life can be very good sometimes.

* * *

Turtle The Wise

Aiiieeee!!! Our grandsons and their grandsons will tell of this day forever. Songs will be sang around the campfires of this day. The day our warriors avenged the Comanche raid before the last snows. Our lodge poles have many Comanche scalps hanging from them. A gift from the Ganh.

Three Apache Arrows

We weren't strong enough yet to raid their villages, so the Ganh brought the Comanche warriors to us. We heard them chase the coyote trickster the Ganh had sent to lure them closer. They rode all the way down the valley to the home of the Ganh before the trickster left his horse and changed into the demon warrior. We had ridden close with our weapons when the demon pulled the Comanches to him on the ground. Our mighty warriors attacked and killed them all. Not one escaped to attack us again. Our home near the Ganh will once more be safe. Life can be very good sometimes.

Chapter 26

"Cap'n Jack, I know we are a prospering cattle outfit with our yearly drives, but what in the hell do we need with a bank safe? We could carry all the cash money we got on hand in a five pound flour sack. And what are we going to do with another wood stove? We got two in the cookhouse, and every house on Three Arrows has one in the kitchen. Are we fixing to open up one of them fancy restaurants like they have in Lincoln?" said Rooster.

Kate was standing on the wagon tongue looking at the safe, stove, and anvil, shaking her head, her face mirroring Rooster's thoughts.

"We have a lot more cash on hand than you know, my friend. Lift that anvil," I said.

Rooster reached into the wagon bed with his good arm and got a grip on the anvil horn. He gave a slow pull, then cocked one of his lanky legs against a wheel and put some muscle into it. It didn't move an inch.

"It ain't nice to play tricks on old crippled cowboys, Cap'n Jack. You got that anvil bolted down good and proper."

"Nope, it's just sitting there."

"Well there ain't nothing that heavy but...nah, you're pulling my leg now."

Katie said, "Jack, is he saying that anvil is made of, of...gold?" she smiled.

I nodded my head. I had asked them to ride to the wagon with me after breakfast. We were all alone with the wagon still parked at the blacksmith shop. An old cowboy, and a beautiful red headed woman were both speechless. That was saying a lot for these two. When they heard the rest of what I had to tell them, they might stay that way.

I climbed in the wagon bed next to the anvil. I reached down with my knife and made a tiny scrape revealing the gold under the black paint.

"Darling, where...?"

"Cap'n, I think you got one hell of a yarn to tell us. That's more gold than a hundred prospectors could mine in a year"

Not saying a word, I walked to the stove and made a second scrape with my knife revealing another gold streak.

"Great gobs of goose grease. There ain't that much gold in the world. I can see why you brought that bank safe," said Rooster.

I walked to the safe and made another scrape.

Katie said, "I think I'm going to faint."

Rooster said, "I think I'm gonna join ya."

Sitting them both down before they did so, I told them the whole thing, from discovering the gold in the butte to the trip back. How I had melted enough of it down to fabricate the safe, stove, and anvil, painting them black to disguise them, and burying the rest. I had them both on the edge of their chairs when I told them about evading the Comanche war party, then I had them bent over laughing when I told them of Vass Hart standing on top of the safe looking for money inside it, and running for his life with the rest of his gang from the same war party. I didn't have to tell them this was a tale they could never repeat. Now they understood the need for secrecy I had exhibited.

"Cap'n Jack, this ranks right up there with one of them Greek tales. How are we gonna hide all this gold? It can't sit on that wagon forever without some cowboys wondering about it."

"Rooster is right, darling. What are we going to do with it?"

"I was thinking of building a wagon barn around it that would be attached to the blacksmith shop. Once we get behind closed doors, I can disassemble the stove and safe into the smaller pieces I welded together. Then it's only a matter of melting it down into brick sized bullion."

"That's a powerful lot of bricks to hide," said Rooster.

"Any ideas?" I asked.

Kate said, "Why not in plain sight?"

Rooster and I looked at each other not understanding.

"A coat of paint worked once, why not again? All the bricks in a wall or a floor look just alike if they are the same size and color." She was right. Rooster and I nodded to each other.

"I see why you married her Cap'n. Understanding why that much money needs to be hid, and don't need to be in the wrong hands, I got the big question to ask. What do we do with it besides hide it?"

It was a question I had been studying on. What does a man do with over a hundred million dollars in gold? No easy solutions. It would have to be handled delicately to prevent any attention to Three Arrows. I would have to make bank deposits in several eastern and San Francisco banks, subtle land investments, maybe some in other countries. Most of the gold could safely stay here as bricks.

We walked our horses back to the ranch house, and discussed the problem most people think they would love to have. I wasn't so sure I did.

"Rooster, do you remember what I said about our safety here?"

"It's a fact of life, Cap'n, you keep you guns loaded and handy every day. No one else here to protect us," said Rooster.

"Nor a doctor to tend to us, no bank to handle money, no dry goods store for supplies, no school, no law. On the other side of the coin, we got more than our share of outlaws and Comanches. The difference in Three Arrows and a town, is more people live in towns, and that brings all those other things because there is safety is in numbers. What makes a town sprout up, Katie?" I said.

"Same things we all want, people, safety, and money of course," she said.

"Right. A lot of towns spring up around a fort on the frontier, and ports, or railroads, to grab a piece of whatever passes through it."

"Fort Sumner is a long way from here, and the closest railroad is hundreds of miles away, Cap'n. Not much of anything flows through this end of New Mexico."

"Only one thing, my friend. Cattle. There is a river of cows flowing through this area ever since Charles Goodnight started that drive with Oliver Loving. What if there was a cattle town right here, where a rancher could sell his herd without depending on a long drive north? We could drive bigger herds north, and one day the railroad might see fit to run a spur line to that town."

I could see Katie's mind working behind her eyes. She is an extraordinary woman with a good head on her shoulders. I'm glad she is my wife. She had a question.

"Darling, you know this area better than any of us. Where would this town be?"

"Three Arrows valley runs south about ten miles before it opens to a wide prairie with plenty of streams running through it. All approaches from the south come together there. It's part of our land and I can't think of a better investment than a town."

"What would you name it, Jack?" she asked.

"Rooster chimed in, "Ain't but one name for it. Shane."

And Shane, New Mexico Territory it was.

Chapter 27

I can't recall seeing Rooster as speechless, or sweating as much as he was now. It was the day Maria and he were going to tie the knot, and his turn to squirm. I was enjoying every minute of it.

"You know, it ain't too late to make a run for it." It was hard to keep a straight face.

"You're a mean one, Cap'n Jack," he said.

"A fast horse might get you out the town gate and up in the Guadalupes before her brothers caught up to you. A man might have a chance in those mountains."

"I'd rather take my chances with Comanches than those brothers. Besides, I want to be remembered as the first man to get hitched in the brand new town of Shane. The first one in this new church building too. They might even put up a statue of me."

Chuckling to myself, I knew wild horses couldn't pull Rooster out of his wedding. Since the Comanche attack, neither he nor Maria would let the other out of sight. They were good people and good for each other. Maria had insisted on waiting until the church was built, so their marriage could be performed in it. Katie understood this better than I did of course, me being just a simple man, and a cowboy to boot.

The surveyors had arrived at the town site about six months ago to lay out the streets and building lots. They were followed by a steady stream of tradesmen and freight wagons. We laid out the center of town around a strong flowing spring of sweet water. The center of the site was a common area of about four acres, with the trees and grass remaining. On one side of the square were; the livery stables, blacksmith shop, a building suitable for a saloon, and the sheriff's office, with rooms for his tenants inside. On the other side, in the middle of the block, was a hotel and restaurant Charley had built to her specifications, as she was going to run it. She had already named it the Shane House. There was also a dry goods store and a lady's apparel shop our old friend Maxie was opening. Doctor Kari had an office on the corner. There were some empty shops built for room to grow. At one end of the square was the location of our bank, and at the other end of town was the church where we now stood. The new cattle pens stood a few hundred yards outside the saloon side of town, as we now called it. Lots for houses were laid out on the other side of town for those who wanted to build one.

"Do you reckon we got time for a glass of sour mash while I'm still a free man?" said Rooster.

Looking at my watch I nodded my head. "We got about an hour before the women get here. Cort and Martin are escorting them and a lot of guests who will be having their first look at our new town."

We walked our horses across the courtyard to the empty building erected for the saloon. I reached in my saddle bag for the liquid courage I brought for the occasion. I poured us a drink in some tin cups, and we stood up to the bar with our foot on the rail.

"How are we going to stock this town with folks, Cap'n?" asked Rooster.

"I figure if we make room and furnish the basic town, it will grow on its own when the cows start coming. C.W. Motes will be bringing a herd next month to sell right here, and it will be part of our drive next spring," I said.

"Cap'n, we were ready to bury Martin after those Indians paid us a visit. Now he's going to be Shane's first sheriff. He still uses a cane, but he is coming around. No sane man would want to brace him, cane or not. Diego was the perfect choice for his deputy. Martin knew what he was doing when he picked him to watch his back. I still can't figure how you stole that smart young lady sawbones, Doc Kari, away from Lincoln."

"It was easy, I just offered her a place to practice medicine with her name on the shingle hanging outside, and all the equipment and medical supplies she needed to get started. As a female sawbones she wants a chance to prove herself," I said.

"Three Arrows is going to get plumb lonely, with all of its people running this town."

"With you managing the ranch, Cort worrying about the herd and ramrodding the hands, and Juan running the farm I reckon I can just retire." I said.

Rooster's head started bobbing up and down, and a noise came out of his throat sounding like he was strangling. He sprayed sour mash whiskey across the bar. His drink must have gone down the wrong way. I slapped him on the back, and he waved me off as the noises coming out of his mouth turned to laughter, and tears were pouring out of his eyes.

"Yep, and we are just gonna fly the cows to the rail head after we paint 'em up like mallards and tell 'em they're ducks." He started whooping again. "Come on Cap'n Jack, let's go get me hitched."

* * *

"Do you, Percival Day Wellington, take Maria Carmen Mancha, to be your lawful wedded wife, to have and to hold, from this day forward, for better or worse, richer or poorer, in sickness and health, to death do you part?" said the preacher, his words echoing in the new church.

My head popped up, along with several others. We had never heard Rooster's Christian name before, but I knew he would be hearing it from us in the future. I caught his eye and mouthed the word, "Percy?" with a smile on my face. He had a look on his face like a deep water Baptist preacher caught in a saloon, but managed to say, "I do," in a confident voice.

Rooster was well liked and there were many neighboring families and most of the Three Arrows hands in attendance. The only hands not present were the ones needed at the ranch. There was also an older couple I didn't recognize. They had to be folks new to the area, or someone who wanted to invest in our new town.

There had been many inquiries about business space and opportunities from cattle brokers and land companies, and even a gypsy fortune teller. The latter promised to predict our future with complete accuracy. She might come in handy.

"I now pronounce you man and wife, you may kiss the bride." Rooster and Maria had the same look between them that Katie and I had at our wedding, and still do.

"Old friend, I want to be the first to shake your hand, and kiss the bride," I said.

"Thank you, thank..." Rooster looked at the back of the church and tears rolled down his face. He led Maria by the hand to the back of the church where the old couple was standing. He embraced them both, then wrapped his arm around Maria, and whispered something to her, then they all embraced. Rooster waved us over.

"Cap'n Jack, Miss Kate, come here quick, I want you to meet my father and mother, Grady and Margaret Wellington, easterners, but fine folks. This may be the best damn day of my life."

"Glad to meet you, sir. Roos... 'uh I mean, Percy, didn't let us know you were coming, or we would have shown you some Three Arrows hospitality," I said.

His mother took my hand and said, "He couldn't tell you because we wanted to surprise him."

"That you did, mother, I sent you a letter, but never expected you make a trip across the country. You done got me acting shy now I'm so surprised," said Rooster.

"Not likely, Percival Day Wellington. You aren't so old I can't grab you by the ear for fibbing." She winked and hooked arms with Maria and Kate. They were swallowed up by a crowd of grinning women speaking both English and Spanish with no apparent problem of communication. Katie would tell me I wouldn't understand it, being a man and all. And she'd be right.

"Grady, occasionally I am a drinking man, are you?"

"Well, since this is a special occasion, Captain." Rooster rolled his eyes at both of us.

"Just call me Jack."

"Alright Jack, lead the way."

Shane, New Mexico Territory, started its first wedding party. Beef was being slow grilled on the square, and Consuelo was directing cooking chores to her many cousins, most of them new arrivals to Shane and Three Arrows. Tables were set up with food and every mouth watered with the smoky aromas of beef and peppers tantalizing the air. Kegs of beer and bottles of sour mash quenched thirsts in the saloon. The sounds of guitars and fiddles tuning up and clicking castanets signaled the start of the fiesta. It would last until the late night hours.

Rooster was getting rode hard about his name by some of the hands in the square. Grady and I sat at a table in the shade of a tall cottonwood toward the end of the square. Here it was possible to talk over the music and noise of the fiesta.

"Jack, I can see the affection Kate and yourself, and all of these good folks feel for my son. Along with his mother, I hoped for many years he would return to our home. Now he's made his own." He paused, and poured himself another drink. "Damn good sour mash. I have a favor to ask, would you mind if Maggie and I extended our visit here?"

"Not at all, I was going to ask you to visit Three Arrows. Looking to the future, Katie and I recently built a large ranch house with plenty of room, and you are welcome to stay with us at our home, or at the least let us offer you a suite at the Shane House if you would prefer."

"Maggie and I would both like to be near the newlyweds. Uh, after tonight of course." We both laughed.

"What line of work are you in, Grady?"

"I am surprised my son didn't tell you. I own a shipping company that operates from the Florida coast to Mexico, and down to South America. Our ships connect in port to local freighting companies, some of which are ours. I was hoping one day that Percy would take the business over, being my only son. After seeing him today, I know in my heart this is his home and Maria is his heart."

Grady looked around him at Americans and Mexicans drinking, laughing, dancing, many of the couples were of mixed blood. "You wouldn't see these people together in the east. White men and negroes are worlds apart, and they speak the same language. Percy and Maria would be ostracized, and so would their children. He and I both would constantly be defending their honor. Here, the difference isn't even thought of."

I smiled, "Folks here know the difference too. It just isn't important when you have struggled and fought for survival together. Wounds from the war with Mexico have healed for the most part, on both sides. There are hotheads from each side of the Rio Grande that hate anyone different from themselves. Those kinds of people will never change, so it's up to the rest of us to raise our children the right way. If you stay here long enough, I promise you will understand and develop a taste for chili peppers too."

Chapter 28

It hurt me to watch one of the deadliest gunmen in the west climb the stairs to the Shane House. He was red in the face and sweating like a horse thief, but he kept on coming, as he always would. He carried his cane in his free hand, and in spite of being in obvious pain, his cold blue eyes never wavered. There was a star pinned to his shirt.

"How is the leg this morning, Martin?" I asked.

"Damned thing feels like I must look. I can't remember stairs this tall and hard to climb. I must be getting old. I've grown to hate this cane." He held it up and examined it, then sat down at my table.

"I reckoned you and it were close friends by now." I poured him a cup of coffee from the pot on the table.

"If you were in my boots, would you want your gun hand holding a wooden stick when you needed iron in it? Damn thing can get me killed. Some drunken cowhand wants to make a name for himself, and I end up shooting it out with a cane." He smiled at this. I wish Rooster was here to hear this. I'm sure he had a similar story, or would in a couple of days. For some reason he wanted to spend all his time at Three Arrows with his new bride. It wouldn't surprise me if there were some *gallitos* running through their house in the future. He was truly *El Gallo* in his barnyard. Maria's sisters and brother adored him. His parents reluctantly ended their visit, and traveled back east a few weeks ago. They promised to return soon and we all hoped they would.

"Martin, I need to come into town more often. I want to meet all the new residents when they arrive, but it ain't been possible with all the work being done at the ranch."

"A lot of folks are digging in here, Cap'n Jack. We finally got the saloon rented by some bar folks that won't tolerate rowdies. A land company moved in the saloon side of the street, and that gypsy fortune teller arrived in her wagon, and set up shop near the stockyards."

"Let's go visit our new citizens."

"Damn, I just got up these stairs and you're ready to go back down. Since I've already visited the saloon a time or two, why don't you go ahead without me. I'll walk over when I finish my coffee, and we can get on with the rest of the visiting."

I nodded to him and got up from the table. I descended the porch stairs and walked across the town courtyard to the saloon. I stepped on the boardwalk and walked through the saloon's batwing doors. The bartender was bent over a keg of beer, tapping it.

"Be right with you, neighbor. Hold that thirst for a minute while I get this spigot in."

The voice was familiar. "Barkeep, why do I get the feeling I know you?"

"I reckon because you do, Cap'n Jack." It was Willie, the bartender from Fort Stockton.

I heard a voice behind me say, "I've been waiting for you to come back to me cowboy, and since you haven't, I decided to come looking for you."

I knew who it was before I turned around, but I wasn't prepared for the sight of her. It was Stormy, every man's dream in a tight blue dress, and wearing a sunshine smile from ear to ear. I had wondered if she was still in Fort Stockton. I had forgotten what a handsome woman she was with that long raven black hair.

"Come here gal and give me a squeeze! Damn, it's good to see you! How did you ever end up here?" I opened my arms and she ran in. Our hug was a little bit tight and lasted a little longer than it should have. I'm not sure if it was Stormy's doing or mine.

"I heard there was a new town opening up in the New Mexico territory named Shane, and I bet Willie you had to be there. Fort Stockton was getting rougher every night, so we loaded up the wagon one morning with all our stock and bar supplies, and here we are. And seeing you, I'm glad we did." She came over and hugged me again.

A shadow filled the door, probably Martin come to fetch me for our walk. I wasn't that lucky.

"Well Captain Shane, I wondered what you were doing in a saloon this early, and now I know." It was Katie.

"You must be Kate, the one this cowboy was lower than a well-digger moping over when I last saw him in Fort Stockton. I hope you have made an honest man out of him by now," Stormy said. She smiled and Katie did too. I could breathe again.

"Yes, as a matter of fact I have, and also a father. Of course that was after he rescued me, and we had a shootout with Mexican bandits." I think I detected the least bit of smug in her voice.

"Jack, it seems like you have been one busy cowboy. Kate, why don't you let Jack go do cowboy things while you and I visit over a pot of tea? I'd like to hear all about these adventures."

I was shooed out the door and glad to be on safer ground. I met Martin walking across the square with a grin on his face.

"She ain't got you by the ear so I guess you don't have to sleep in the livery tonight."

"Matter of fact, she caught me hugging Stormy Jones."

"The hell you say!" Martin looked wide-eyed at me.

"An old friend is all. I left her and Kate tea huddling. By dinnertime Stormy will know what color the house curtains and my underwear are, and Kate will know every step I took in Fort Stockton a couple of years ago," I said.

"Women are like that for a fact. Instant friends or instant cat fights, if they think the other has eyes for her man. I decided long ago it was safer chasing outlaws than gals. I'm not sure I could outdraw a pretty one if I was looking at her and my thinking was somewhere it shouldn't be."

"You're in rare form today, Martin. You remind me of a fellow I know named Rooster," I said.

"That's good company anytime. Here we are, Cap'n. This is our new tenant's land company office."

I looked up at the sign over the door and laughed out loud. It read: M & W Land Company.

"Martin, I had to teach these swindlers a lesson a couple of years ago in Lincoln. They were in cahoots with a crooked tax clerk, and stealing farms for the back taxes supposedly owed on them." I was going to enjoy this.

My old friends the carpetbaggers. Lincoln must have run them out of town on a rail. I entered their office door without knocking.

The tall one named Wayne greeted me with a glad handshake and said, "Good morning sir, I can see you are an enterprising man such as...oh no, it's you!"

"Boys, what are you doing in my town? And when I say, "My town," that is literal. I own this town including this building and the land it is built on. Do you need directions out of town?"

"Mister Shane, I'm sorry our last mutual endeavor didn't materialize, but surely we can make amends. Mister Michael and myself don't have much cash on hand, but we do now own a substantial parcel of a thousand acres that is rumored to be rich in gold ore. We purchased it from a ranch near here for...I believe it was a hundred dollars an acre, and as a gesture of good will, we would be glad to let you buy in for a piece, or all of it if you like."You could see the wheels turning in his head. These two never gave up. It was my turn.

"Boys, whose name was on the claim you bought this thousand acres from?"

"Why it was the Three Arrows ranch wasn't it Mister Michael?"

Mister Michael nodded his head and said, "Fine, fine ranch. Loaded with integrity. It reminds me of our own M & W Land Company."

Martin started coughing behind me. He caught on quick.

"I see, and did you ever get around to meeting the owner of this ranch?" I said.

"Not personally, the bank in Lincoln handled the transaction," said Mister Wayne, a shade of doubt in his voice.

"Gentlemen, allow me to introduce myself. Captain Jack Shane, as in Shane, New Mexico Territory and the owner of the Three Arrows ranch. I happen to know for a fact you spent fifty dollars an acre for that land, not a hundred. To show you I'm a fair man I will buy it back from you for ten dollars an acre, and that's twice what it's worth."

"Well now, that land has some valuable oil and tar deposits that would bring a pretty penny back east," Mister Michael said.

"That's true. There is a market for kerosene and grease there, and I hear they are using tar to pave some roads. The only problem with that figuring is that market is over two thousand miles from here, and they already have plenty of it there. Boys, that ten thousand dollar offer will turn into five thousand this afternoon. Either way your business is done here. There will be a check for you and papers to sign at the bank until noon"

I had the rats cornered, but I wasn't worried about a fight. Their kind usually know when they are beaten. I really was being generous at ten dollars an acre for desert land that nothing would grow on with those tar and oil deposits. But who knows, it might be worth something someday.

There was no mistaking which wagon belonged to the gypsy fortune teller. The tall wooden wagon was parked in the shade of a hackberry tree. It was brightly painted, and carved in the wood were ornamental symbols and designs I could only guess at the meaning of. Red and yellow stairs led to a door on the front of the wagon. A sign above the door was painted with the legend: *Madam Love, Reveals Destiny and Romance, Only One Dollar.* There was a row of red hearts and question marks around the border of the sign. This was definitely a business woman.

I knocked on the door and a raspy voice on the other side said, "Enter, and be enlightened."

Behind me, Martin said, "These steps are so pretty I hate to step on them, Cap'n." We climbed the steps and entered a small sitting area with a table in the middle of it. Martin and I each took a chair, and gazed around us at the ornamental artwork. I don't know much about art, but it looked European and old. The curtains at the rear of the wagon parted, and an old gypsy woman slowly made her way to the table. She used a cane with a silver handle to steady herself. She was as colorful as the wagon with her clothes and shawls. She wore a veil over her face and a turban with a blue feather stuck in it on her head.

"Are you seekers of destiny, or is this a social visit, gentlemen?" she asked.

"A man always wants to know what lies around the next bend. I'm Captain Jack Shane and this is Martin Cold, the town sheriff. We wanted to meet you, and welcome you to Shane," I said.

"Greetings. May I see your palm sheriff?"

Martin handed her his left hand. He didn't like his right one encumbered. She held it and studied his palm, tracing the lines with a fingernail. Martin watched intently.

"Hmmmm, I see a lot of violence in your life. There has been some recently, perhaps from Indians. I can see more strife and violence in your future. Perhaps you should leave this area."

Martin withdrew his hand like it had been burned. She reached for mine next. I gave it to her. She examined it as she had Martin's.

"You have recently acquired a large sum of money. You will also lose it, and come to regret your treatment of someone in your past." She looked up from my hand for a moment then her raspy voice continued, "I have more bad news for you, Captain. You will soon lose someone close to you that you love dearly. I am sorry to bring you these tidings of gloom, but I promise you, all of this is true." That was enough for me. I pulled my hand from hers.

"I guess we got our dollar's worth, Martin. Thank you for your time, Madam Love."

"No charge, gentlemen. The first reading for you is free. My way of saying thank you for the welcome."

We left the wagon and walked back the way we had come. Martin was the first to speak.

"You didn't buy any of those cow patties that smelly old woman was selling did you, Cap'n?"

"Of course not. I'm wondering why she didn't tell us we were going to have good fortune since she was making it up as she went along. It wouldn't have cost her anything."

"I can speculate on that. When I pulled my hand back her veil slipped a little, and I could see her face a little better. That is one ugly woman who doesn't much like herself. If I had a horse that ugly I might have to shoot it." This got us both to laughing. I still had a funny feeling in the pit of my stomach. She had been too close to the truth.

We walked back across the square to the Shane House for another pot of coffee. Charley stood on the porch waving for us to hurry, and from her demeanor her feathers were ruffled about something. Her hair was askew, and she kept turning her head to look over her shoulder. I wonder if she had been to the gypsy and had her fortune read.

"Unka Jack, Unka Martin, help! I'm flustered! Cort brought the boys to town, and he's run off somewhere leaving me to chase both of them, and I have to run things here, and go to the dry goods store, and make sure the beds are made, and the kitchen is..."

"Whoa, Charley." I took the stairs two at a time to the porch, and hugged her. I held her tight, as I had when she was a child. She relaxed and looked up at me smiling.

"You always make things alright, Unka Jack."

"Don't worry, Martin and I will watch the boys for a couple of hours while you catch up."

"Oh, thank you, thank you." We both got hugs and kisses, and Charley handed me the boys. One for each arm. Poor Martin, he had reached the porch and had to descend the steps again. We walked to his office and carried the boys to a cell. We spread a blanket on the floor, and gave them some wooden bowls and spoons to play with. They were soon making contented noises.

"Watch this Cap'n." Martin removed some bullets from his gun belt, and flipped one of them to Garrett. His tiny hand shot out like a rattlesnake, snagging the bullet.

"Now watch this." He flipped a bullet to Austin. He didn't catch it, but knocked it down and picked it up in a tiny fist.

"Try to take that bullet from Austin and you'll have to use both hands. That other little outlaw has the fastest reflexes I ever saw in a child. We played this game a lot while I was healing, and Garrett never misses a catch. One fast, one strong. A fine pair of boys."

We spent a couple of hours talking horses, and enjoying the boys until Charley came with a wagon to take them home to

Three Arrows. Cort had already returned to the ranch to handle a situation with some rowdy cowboys. Arguments over who was the best roper or rider or marksman were best derailed before they went from fistfights to gunplay.

We sat outside the jail watching the wagons and riders go by, and I thought again about the fortune teller's prophesy, and dismissed it. Hard times and bad news came along often enough without imagining more of it.

Katie brought our horses. We told Martin goodbye and set out for Three Arrows. It was a nice afternoon, and being in no hurry, we let the horses walk at their own speed.

"Jack, may I ask you a question?" said Kate.

"Sure, sweetheart," I said.

"Do you think Stormy is pretty?"

"In her way I suppose she is." Why did she ask that? I didn't like the direction this was going.

"What way is that?"

"You know, she's got kind of nice hair and a nice face." I knew I was going to step on a rattlesnake if I wasn't careful. Katie smiled, and I knew what she was up to.

"Jack, you're a terrible liar, but I love it. I'm pulling your tail."

I saw something ahead of us in the middle of the road. I hoped it wasn't what I thought it was. I put heels to my horse and cantered ahead. I was right about what it was, and wished I wasn't. It was Charley's wagon, and it was empty. Where were she and the boys? The gypsy's words haunted me.

Chapter 29

We found Charley. She was unconscious, lying face down and covered in blood. The ground was kicked up around her and her dress had been ripped. She had put up a hell of a fight. I picked her up gently and carried her to the wagon. Katie was riding in circles calling Garrett and Austin. They were gone.

I said, "Katie, ride for Three Arrows! Tell Cort to grab everyone there and search for the boys. Maybe they wandered toward home. I'm taking Charley to Doc Kari as fast as I can get there. I'll come back here with Martin, and we'll pick up their trail."

"Find our children Jack, and bring them home. Then I want you to kill the son of a bitch who took them!" Her Irish temper was roaring as mine was. God help the man who took our boys and did this to Charley.

She turned her roan and galloped toward Three Arrows. I tied my horse to the wagon, and drove the team back to town as fast they could run. It was a rough ride in the back of the buckboard, but Charley knew nothing of it if she were still alive. I reigned in hard and used the foot brake to stop in front of Doc Kari's office. She saw me lift Charley out of the wagon, and helped me get her inside on a bed. I wanted to ride back and search for the boys, but I made myself stay while the doctor examined her. She might provide a clue to the boys' whereabouts.

"Whoever did this to her needs to be shot! She will recover, Captain, but this woman was pistol whipped. She got her licks in too from the look of her hands. There is skin under those fingernails. This was done by a big man, and it was personal."

"When she comes to, Doc, tell her I've gone for the boys." I had explained the situation to her during the examination.

"Captain," she paused, "shoot the bastard that did this." I nodded, and ran for the sheriff's office.

Minutes later, Martin and I were on the road to Three Arrows. Diego was alerting Spanish town, and Maxie was spreading the word throughout the rest of town. Soon there would be people looking under every rock for any sign of them. Stormy closed the saloon, and Willie, her, and their customers joined the hunt.

Martin and I were both good trackers, and soon picked up a trail leading away from the spot where we found Charley and the wagon. There appeared to be only one horseman and he was carrying a load. Garrett and Austin.

The trail led back to Shane, and it appeared there had been no attempt to hide it. As we neared town, the ground became muddier and merged with the cattle trails leading to the stockyards. It was impossible to follow the trail through the thousands of cow tracks in front of us. We rode the trail again to see if they had backtracked, but found no sign. They had gone to Shane.

There was only one person who hated us enough to kidnap our children. He had disappeared in a sandstorm with Comanches after his scalp. It had been wishful thinking on my part to assume his hair was hanging on a lodge pole in Comancheria. The only man evil enough to pistol whip a woman, and steal our children was Vass Hart. And I knew where he was.

* * *

Three Apache Arrows

Vass Hart

I knew he'd figure it out and come for me. Exactly what I wanted you to do, almighty Captain Jack Shane. A cattle empire, a town named after you, and a wagon load of gold I know you got hid somewhere. You can keep the cows and town, but that gold is mine. You can thank me for that pretty red headed wife you got too. If I hadn't come along and taken out her husband, she would be long gone and you wouldn't have her.

You don't know it, but I was hot on your heels in the desert before you gave us the slip with that gold. Hadn't been for those damn Comanches, I would have caught you. I still want to ask you: what in the name of hell you were doing with a wood stove and a bank safe in the middle of the desert? Rafe and Cliff made it out of that dust storm with me and are waiting in Mexico. Them other fellows though, they went out hard when the Indians caught them.

The Comanche are a cruel people, but a man could learn a lot from them on how to get revenge on someone. It was something to think on when I was riding back to the wagon with these boys. Two of them were too much for me to carry on horseback, so when I saw some Indians I set one of them on the ground, and put the spurs to my horse. That was his bad luck.

Of course I made sure the one I kept was your pup, Captain. I got plans for him. Sorry I didn't get to spend a little more time with that niece of yours. I wanted to carve her up a little as payment for her damned claw marks, among other things. I did bloody her after she turned wildcat on me and scratched me to pieces. I think I may have killed her with my last blow to her head. If not, well, I may pass this way again someday.

They are almost here and I guess I need to be sociable, me and the little captain will go outside to meet them.

* * *

Captain Jack

It was dark when we rode up to the gypsy wagon and dismounted. There was a lantern outside. He expected visitors. The wagon door opened and Vass Hart stepped out with Garrett under his arm. He was grinning, and held a knife to my son's throat.

I heard a low growl come from my mouth, and readied myself for a charge. A hand gripped my shoulder. I turned to see Martin shake his head.

One look at Martin's face stopped the outlaw in his tracks. The cold blue eyes and death's head grimace was enough to freeze your blood. Vass Hart knew who he was, and that the only reason he was alive was the fact he was holding Garrett.

I sensed another presence beside me. I turned, and there was, Maxie. I would remember him standing by us this day.

"Captain Jack Shane, come to visit. Do you believe your fortune now?" He laughed in the raspy voice of the old gypsy woman. "When did you figure it out?"

"When you got a little too smart with the sign on your wagon. Hearts and question marks. Spelled different, but sound the same. If you had gone on your way, I might never have thought about it again. Nobody, but a sick man like you, would take children from their parents and pistol whip a woman. Where is the other boy?" I asked.

"Don't rightly know, the last I saw of him he was about to meet some Indians. I heard they like some young'uns, but others they just...well you know, " Hart's voice trailed off.

Garrett started squirming and tried to pull the handle on

Hart's sidearm in the holster. He swapped the boy to his other arm. Martin watched him closely for the split second he needed to draw and shoot. Hart was visibly nervous.

Maxie tugged at my sleeve and said, "I think I can get your son out of this safely if you will agree to let Hart be hung another day. You have to trust me on this"

As much as I wanted Hart dead a hundred times over, I wanted my son safe more. I nodded to Maxie, having no idea what he had in mind. He pulled out paper and pencil, and hastily wrote something. He folded the paper and said, "Vass, if I can get you on that horse alone and out of here alive will you go?"

"You and me both know that ain't going to happen, Maxie. Those two killers over there want me bad. What crazy idea you got in mind?"

"Read this and tell me if you want me to post this on the town board, or do you want to ride out of here alive and alone?" He handed Vass the folded paper he had written on. The muscles in Hart's face flexed and he grit his teeth. A stream of curses came out of his mouth that made me glad Garrett wasn't old enough to understand it.

"I told you I'll kill you if you ever tell this. Do you think I changed my mind?"

"Yeah Vass, I'm just as afraid of you as I always was, but I can't let you hurt a child. I know this will stop you, and Captain Jack has agreed to give you safe passage out of town if you let the boy go. And nothing on that paper will get out, you have my word."

"What about The Iceman? I ain't holding his boy."

I looked at Martin, and he nodded his agreement.

I thought it was going to go easy, but there was too much hate in Vass Hart.

"Sounds good to me gents," he stepped down the stairs holding Garrett under one arm,and his knife in the other hand. His horse was tied to the stair rail. He swung his leg over the saddle and untied the reins. He got a sick look on his face I had seen before and grinned.

"I got to leave you something to remember me by." He swapped arms with Garrett and turned him bottom side up. "My mark cut in his backside will do for a brand." He was going to put his knife to my son, knowing we couldn't shoot for fear of hitting the boy, but Garrett had grabbed Hart's sidearm again. This time by the trigger guard.

"Hey, damn you brat, let that go!" Hart made the mistake we were waiting for and yanked Garrett up from his side. Garrett's little hand had already grabbed the trigger.

KABLOOM! Vass Hart shot his own kneecap off with my son assisting. The gunshot and Hart's screams spooked his horse, and he bucked like he was being branded. Garrett was thrown in the air, and the horse raced into the dark with the outlaw on his back screaming in agony. I dove for Garrett. My elbows hit the ground and I caught him in my hands. Martin and Maxie fired their pistols in the dark hoping for a lucky shot. I lay on the ground holding my son. He was laughing.

The ride from the gypsy wagon to Doc Kari's wasn't far. I dreaded the fact I might find Charley dead, and if not, what I would have to tell her about Austin. Martin and Maxie flanked me for support. I wasn't prepared for what I found.

Rooster met me at the door holding an Indian child. It wasn't an Indian, it was Austin! After what Vass Hart had told us I didn't know if I would ever see him again.

Rooster saw me gawking, and said, "Same way I felt when I first saw him. Take a look at this." He opened the top of the small tunic Austin was wearing, revealing a necklace.

It was the necklace Charley had made years ago, from the three arrowheads I brought home from the canyon. She had tied it around Austin's neck for good luck. It must have worked.

"Two Apache squaws came to the ranch house with him before dark. Kate and Cort took him from them, and sent them home with bacon, flour, and all the other food they could carry. I think we made some friends when we sent them steers when they was beat down by the Comanches."

Kate came through the door reaching for Garrett. She looked me in the eye and said, "Did you shoot him?"

I said, "No, Garrett did." Her mouth dropped and formed a surprised smile.

I heard a familiar voice from inside. "Unka Jack, did he really? Can Austin shoot him too?"

I looked inside at my niece and knew she was going to be her sassy self again.

Sometimes life can be very good.

Epilogue

Stormy brought us a bottle of my favorite sour mash whiskey from the saloon's storeroom. Martin, Maxie, Rooster, and I sat in the private room behind the bar.

"I tried to pick up Hart's sign at first light. I followed his blood trail for a half mile or better before it petered out in the mud. He must have wrapped something around that knee," said Martin.

We all started laughing. We couldn't help it. It started every time we thought about Garrett pulling the trigger on Vass Hart's pistol.

"Most likely, he will head towards the border thinking we are on his trail. No need for us to follow. If he makes it across the desert there's some bad men on the border with no love for him. His partners, Rafe and Cliff, probably went under, or quit him. Not much loyalty in an outlaw's camp. Either way, I doubt we'll ever see or hear from Vass Hart again," I spoke with more certainty than I felt. I would never feel comfortable until I knew for sure he was in the grave.

Martin said, "Maxie, when we showed up at that gypsy wagon last night, you did too. How did you know that was where Vass Hart was holed up? And what was written on that piece of paper strong enough for him to surrender Garrett? Not counting the gunshot of course."

We all laughed again until we had tears in our eyes. The

whiskey and the good humor gave us a warm glow, and made the evening surrender its chill.

Maxie appeared to collect his thoughts then began to speak, "Friends, I gave my word not to reveal what was on that piece of paper. My word is my bond, and rather than compromise myself, let me repeat a story I was told a long time ago. It's about a boy.

Many years ago, there was a wealthy couple of Russian descent living back east. They had five children, the youngest of which was the only boy, born later in their life, thus giving him four older sisters who loved to torment him as older sisters are prone to do.

Unfortunately, his father passed away soon after he was born. The mother's sister, who was rumored to be a countess in the old country, came to live with them. She soon adored her nephew, and was very protective of him.

The sisters were jealous of this attention to their brother, and one of their favorite pastimes, was to dress the poor boy as a girl, and pretend he was their little sister. The aunt decided the only way to end the boy's embarrassment was to beat them at their own game. She dressed the boy in expensive girl's clothes, and applied make up, French perfume, and a beautiful blond wig. He was beautiful. Much more so than his homely sisters. They became more jealous. The aunt and mother were so enamored with the new little doll the aunt had created, they arranged for him to play parts written for a young girl, in the theater. He was highly successful, soon becoming a favorite of the theater crowd. This enraged the sisters. To rub it in, or maybe he liked it, he started wearing the theater dresses at home. Not because he wanted to be a female, but because it was a symbol of power.

The story should end here, as children normally grow up and go their separate ways, with all sibling rivalries forgotten. Unfortunately, this was not to be. One day, the sisters finally became too envious and angry. They literally dragged the boy to the basement while the mother and aunt were at market. They stripped him naked and tied him to the ceiling beams. They spent the day torturing him with burning matches held to his flesh, then ripped his dresses to pieces in front of him. When they finally released him, threatening him to tell their mother and aunt of what they had done, he wasn't able to talk, and stared straight ahead as if he was in a trance. The sisters were delighted with what they had done.

There was a fire of mysterious origin that night. It burned the house to the ground.

Only the boy and his aunt escaped alive. They disappeared into the south, and that is where the story ends. His aunt, the countess, was called Vas, which is Russian for royalty. The family's last name was Hartov. Coincidence? I do not know.

What I do know, is a certain rancher's niece purchased a beautiful dance hall dress from me a few years ago that a certain man also wanted to purchase. He was furious at her because of it. I also had a burglary at my dress shop a few nights ago which got me to thinking who might be interested in my wares. There was only one newcomer, an old gypsy. When I heard about Charley and the kidnappings, I was sure of Hart's new identity."

We all sat there for a few minutes not saying anything. We sipped our whiskey and pondered the story we had just heard.

Rooster pulled his Colt out of the holster and opened the cylinder.

"What's that for, Rooster? We are all friends here," I said.

"Thought I better take the bullet out from under the hammer. I don't want to have an accident, and end up shooting myself in the knee."

That lightened the moment and rekindled the laughter.

Life can be very good sometimes.

* * *

"Armando, who is the woman in the wagon? She is very ugly and smells bad. Have you gotten married again?" The bandit chuckled and stepped down from the wagon.

"I found her in the desert; someone has shot her in the leg. I do not think she will live but who knows, there may be a reward if someone is looking for her. Mi buena suerte, no?"

The End

CPSIA information can be obtained at www.ICGtesting.com
Printed in the USA
LVOW04s0717070715

445180LV00001B/1/P